EdenDust

by

BROTHER EDEN DOUGLAS

To ALL My Spiritual Brothers
Past and Future
for their

inspiration

TABLE of CONTENTS

~:~

BOOK ONE

BOOK TWO

BOOK THREE

BOOK FOUR

2010 – EdenDust Publishing
EDENintheDESERT
Albuquerque, NM 87106
www.EdenDust.com

BOOK ONE
Prologue:

I ask you to simply go with me.

I am asking you to understand just a little of my mindset as I began to write this, imagine this ...live this novel. I can't tell you 'when' I got the idea, exactly. But it feels a part of me, symbiotically I know I'm linked to it, obviously, but it's deeper than just being its author.

Just go with me on this journey.

Backwards in time or forward even.., maybe it's a parallel universe where another choice was made. All I know for sure is, 'this isn't it'. This world we have come to accept as our reality no longer feels real to me. It feels overwhelmingly like a mistake. An error that's always attempting to correct itself but ultimately never can 'because the whole world we've come to know is simply a mistake. A very bad experiment gone terribly wrong. I'm writing more out of necessity than desire. I'm writing myself sane you might say. I have always felt a little peculiar, slightly out of place, and time, and I've longed for someone to help me find my way out of this darkness that has become my life. You wouldn't recognize my depression that's masked as boredom, mostly, 'cause I have successfully maneuvered through this life's maze without revealing my true feelings, hiding in plain sight, while I secretly desired for another place to call my home. While countries fought wars over sovereignty, I switched channels, surfing for any bit of escapism I could find. When nothing presented itself on TV, I read volumes of literature always in search of a home in a distant galaxy, praying secretly to find my place of belonging in the stars. Hell ...anywhere, but here in this God forsaken land we call earth. There it was, in that last statement.., God forsaken earth. That's how I've felt for all of my life. I've heard the sermons, listened to the teachers, search the books on faith from all the myriad of religions and they all seem to blindly accept that story of creation as fact. But what if that was the first lie and everything else beyond that fateful exit from EDEN is this world we now live in...and secretly despised? If the alternate universe theory holds true, then there is a place where another choice was made. No not a place where Eve said to the serpent, "nevermind", but a place where Adam never confessed 'loneliness'. A place where being in EDEN, alone with God, was not only pleasurable, but desirable and everything else was borne out of that continuum. Suddenly, you too feel a sense of belonging, don't you? Everything 'wrong' came from that fateful sleep and the 'removal' of something man already had in him to create something outside of himself that he never needed, but only desired. What does a world look and feel like, that was truly designed by GOD, for GOD? Adam never got to experience that place..., at the least the Adam of our lore. But, there is another Adam who made a different choice and he is called by the name of the elements from which he was created.

His name is **...EdenDust**.

...from the Dust of EDEN, *again.*

I've never had anything to compare it to, but I'm told by my angelic brothers that this garden is the most beautiful destination in all the worlds. I could possibly understand how Adam might wish to see beyond the boundaries of EDEN, but how could he leave this place, *and GOD*, with a lesser created thing? In all fairness, I know he was banished, but even in his departure, what upset our Father most was he never even looked back at his original home. Knowing this story from the moment of my awakening, I vowed then and there to never leave EDEN or disappoint my Father.., and I never have.

My birth came in the very same day Adam chose to deceive my Father. The garden started to lose its vitality because its keeper had not chosen it above the woman. Knowing that all that He had created was in mortal jeopardy, My Father lovingly restored the balance by creating another from the sacred dust of EDEN, and breathed life for a second time, into me. They called me EdenDust for the place of birth and as a reminder that this place and I are *ONE*. In every way I am like the first, but for one thing, I know of him and he never knew of me.

I came into existence with all the knowledge that Adam possessed. I knew the name of things that he had named and they recognized by Lordship, instantly. I have another distinction, too, that I would come to understand in time. I was created in possession of the knowledge of Good and evil so that I could never be tempted in such a rudimentary fashion as my predecessor. The gifts and attributes that would have been his, in time, were given to me in the beginning. My Father bestowed upon me all that He had originally wanted for Adam, but withheld. Many times I've wanted to ask Him 'why' He chose to wait especially knowing the presence of the evil that He had allowed in the garden, but no one questions GOD, especially after what we had witnessed in his dealings with Adam, and before that, Lucifer.

LUCIFER. I find it hard to understand, again, how one so beloved by GOD would choose this world over Heaven? But once again, in all fairness, he was banished from Heaven and cast down here, wasn't he? His presence in the garden was inevitable, being given dominion over all this world, but why GOD allowed him near his beloved creation was a mystery until I realized, *'he was never allowed to directly communicate with Adam'*. The woman was a mere shadow of all that Adam inherently possessed and that connection was enough to allow GOD to fully test the remaining integrity of Man as his essence is distributed in his offspring. Possessing the knowledge of Good and evil has allowed me to understand my Father all the more and his actions have always been benevolent even when viewed by others as cruel. Walking with Him in the garden in the cool of the evening is such a time of rejuvenation that I continue to learn of His Ways after all these countless centuries we've shared.

TIME, as we live it in the garden, is different for us than for those outside the gate. We know of their troubles and we see them age and die. There is no death in the garden. The tree of Life is here which also means we don't experience sickness. We know of all these things, but experience none of them. Our joy and peace is eternal. My Loving Father still wants this for all those extensions of his original creation, but for them they must choose it for themselves. We are saddened here by the multitude through the centuries that do not choose Life. Another mystery wrapped in an enigma, one of them coined, but we see it more simply, *they have never been shown the True Nature and Love of Our Father*. Even when my brother Jesus walked among them, He was shunned, despised and called a heretic, for simply being who He was. Seems this fallen version of Man has chosen fear and deceit as its modus operandi and GOD can never be fully viewed with a dark heart. I have asked my Father if I can help them, in any way He deemed necessary and He has said that the time and place of the revelation of my existence is already written and I must be patient. So while I wait, I've decided that to be fully prepared for whatever task I might be called upon to complete, I should recall all I've learned about this place called earth in my observations of this world as it's transformed through the ages. I understand that I share a unique vantage point and a view of GOD that just might be of service to The Trinity being the only one of them, today, that is fully Man.

Yes, I will tell the story that no one has been able to write about life in EDEN, after the fall of the first Man. I long to reveal the ultimate Truth about my Father, and I must prepare for that moment in time when I'm allowed to let the world know what God had originally planned for us all. I believe that time will be soon, but for now, these pages will exist as a testimony in my own hand and, God willing, be read by those chosen secondarily for this prophetic role, if not me.

In the meantime, I will write.

...a Day in EDEN

I'm smiling because that's all there is here..., DAY. With GOD as our constant presence, there is no night. So the first thing I must share is that time is continuous. When I said that GOD walks with me in the cool of the evening, it's actually a very interesting dynamic. In order for me to be in His Presence, He chooses to be less brilliant and that dimming nature feels like evening and the coolness that accompanies his lesser brilliance is soothing. This place of His creation is vast. Our walks through the centuries have never been in the same place, twice. We exist in a world void of limitations, in the moment that GOD wishes it so, it is. Fully realized vistas appear as the norm for us, here, and it's not startling or a miracle as fallen Man would see them, just simple occurrences. GOD is always creating. I know in your texts you read that He rested on the sixth day of creation and called everything Good, as if to imply everything that is and would be was done in those original epochs you call days. He 'rested', but He never stopped creating. If only you could see what He's done since Adam took his last walk through this place. Of all the destinations that Man has created, that they desire to see with their own eyes, that they labor so hard to vacation in, none of that comes close to a simple snapshot in any direction of EDEN at any time and our vistas change consistently and each is more beautiful than the last. I understand that I can't compare it to anything that you've experienced because I've only known what I now see before me, but my beautiful winged brothers come back with reports all the time to us about the state of the fallen world, without the true presence of GOD. I can hardly breathe when I think of what that must feel like. But I digress...

You've noticed by now that I often write 'We' and 'Us'. As a point of fact, I'm the last created Man from the dust and my lineage has not yet begun. I believe that beginning is also part of the appointed place and time my Father refers to. It's my personal belief and hope that I be revealed as part of the New Earth, that's been prophesied. As a side note, I should tell you, now, that The Book of Revelation is the only one of your texts that is completely accurate. As hard as that may be to accept, you must believe me, John passed through here as he was allowed to glimpse into that future realm. I will tell you, also, that I'm referenced in those texts too, which is why I believe as I do about the time of my revelation. I promise to write more specifically on that later.

But I am not alone in EDEN. Besides the continual presence of the Trinity (My Father, GOD; My Brother, Jesus; and My Constant Guardian, The Holy Spirit), there are the heavenly hosts that visits with us when GOD is fully present; the angelic hosts that protects us, the blessed souls that pass through EDEN in route to their heavenly homes, and all present in EDEN collectively share information in a thought, so one's knowledge becomes common knowledge and our joy continually expands because of our connection to one another. Every moment is a unique experience and none compare to the ones that came before it. We simply exist, now. Only I, Man, in my direct connection to the Trinity, possess the ability of what you might call total recall. That's why it's important that I write. I am the only one chosen to record it all. If I were to ask about Adam, the singular Man that left the garden, the hosts only would hear Adam, the fallen state of mankind because everything they're able to share is happening right now. I 'remember' it all and have the ability to separate present from past as you live it, but my viewing of all of life and its events is *continuous*. My *day* in EDEN is beyond your average lifetime and then some. We've seen wars began and end in an instant. We've seen the advancements in technology you toil over, then celebrate, pass as we simply glance in another direction.

Yes, a day in EDEN.

I can't stop smiling.

...in the Presence of GOD

To fully grasp my existence in EDEN, I must begin with my Father. But how do I explain GOD to those that have been so misled by others claiming to know Him?

Jesus, even with His unique bond to the Father, couldn't adequately do it. Most refused to hear Him, or believe in Him and proved to be more comfortable creating a GOD of limitations to match their understanding than to learn from Jesus, firsthand, who GOD really is. There seems to be a ruling class at all times on your earth that has commanded complete knowledge and understanding of GOD and have become a sort of gatekeeper to all information of the contrary. They alone have decided which books are 'good' books of knowledge and which are heretical, often on a pure speculative basis and more often because of their own limited enlightenment. Even more insidious than that are those whose agendas are purely political, often controlling others through religion to remain powerful and influential in ways that mostly benefit their own financial interests. The ones most hurt naturally by their actions are those with real faith, and that truly come into their congregations to learn of GOD but often find themselves shunned as fanatical because their presence exposes the hidden motives of those in power. So, to truly and fully introduce to you my Father, you will have to unlearn most of what you've been taught. Allow me to elaborate.

It's not true that 'no man' has seen GOD and lived. Adam and I are proof of that. But Adam's connection to GOD was severed and GOD could never share his true self any longer with fallen Man as a result of that broken bond, so from the very beginning of your world, Man has struggled to reconnect to GOD. GOD desires that connection, too, but in order to establish it He has to create it in a myriad of unorthodox ways because of His Holiness. That is why He chose to reveal himself as He did to Moses, Noah, Ezekiel and a host of others, for example, by appearing in a burning bush, through the elements as they were, but never face to face. Because of this limitation to see GOD for themselves, man has chosen to *interpret* GOD and pass those interpretations along as fact. The only ones that can dispute or disprove any of this erroneous information are those of us that truly know Him and see Him as He is, I propose.

So let's talk about **GOD**.

In His Presence is Fullness of JOY.
That's the most accurate foundation I can begin with. I know so many have written that when they see GOD or Jesus, they have things to say to them, to get off their chests.., 'bones' to pick with them. Forget about all that nonsense. In their presence, you'll be overcome by and overwhelmed with pure JOY; unspeakable, full of Glory. Trust me on this. It's the most euphoric high you can imagine and then some and all the while you're amazingly lucid and clearly focused. Your complete mind, body (more on this later) and soul are synchronized in passion and praise.

At the apex of that JOY is **LOVE**.

This isn't a warmness in your chest sort of Love, a stirring in your groins love (remember, I have all knowledge of Good and evil), nor a decisive Love determined by your mental or emotional capacity to love. This LOVE is an immediate, mirror reflection of the LOVE being bestowed upon you. Here, my brother John shared with you another truth; GOD is LOVE and even more importantly, LOVE is GOD. Forget what you've been told about a vengeful GOD. That's man interpreting GOD, again, with their limited minds and bias understandings. GOD does nothing from a place that isn't LOVE. *EVERYTHING* He's ever done ...especially His allowance of Jesus to the earth to die in your place for the mortal sin of Adam is nothing but LOVE. A vindictive GOD would never have allowed Adam to leave EDEN. How simple it would have been to just return him to the dust from which he was created and yet, He didn't! Think of all those that's challenged GOD for various mundane reasons and who lived to write about their folly. Those times that Man interpreted GOD as cruel, were simply times that Man failed to get a desired result from GOD, as if He exists only to serve Man. In order to fully comprehend that your very existence is nothing but LOVE, you would have to know that even fallen man is still Good because everything GOD has created is Good. I'll let you meditate on that one for a moment.

All GOOD.

Now you're beginning to understand just why there's so much confusion in your world. You're constantly mislabeling Good for evil and when you do, you then have to create reasons to justify your labels and unfortunately GOD takes the blame for your own limited hearts. To know GOD as I do, you can never come before Him with a shadow of doubt in your heart about His Goodness. What was the mistake of Adam? Was it that he listened to his lesser self and was deceived? No, Adam's misstep was that he 'hid' himself from GOD which meant for the first time ever, he had 'doubt' in his heart about GOD. Doubt is the precursor to Fear and Fear is the direct opposite of LOVE. Adam was banished because he failed to continue to LOVE GOD with all his being and his actions proved that he no longer believed GOD could love him. All of those leaders and teachers on earth that so very often preach about the GOD of retribution have never known my Loving Father and the shame of it all is your world continues to fail to do your own research for fear of being labeled a misguided heretic or worse, *sinful.*

SIN. What an overused, abused and misunderstood word. How much have you been told is sin?

In fact, it would be easier for you to name what isn't sin, I suppose. What comes to your mind right now, that isn't sin? Everything Good created has been labeled sin by one group or the other and depending on your personal sin guilt, there are sins that are unforgivable, unredeemable ...unlovable. This might be Lucifer's greatest contribution to mankind. He has robbed you consistently of knowing the fullness of your earthly experience by getting you to deny yourself of all that God has created for you.

The easiest way to accomplish this was to call every 'good' thing, bad. When Jesus walked amongst you, this was the underlying theme of all the challenges to His Authority and Deity. They challenged who Jesus preached to, when He preached, even, where he preached.., always presenting Him with what was clearly defined to them, as the sinful acts He committed willingly according to their Laws. In the story of the woman presented to Him caught in the act of adultery, why did Jesus ask those without sin to cast the first stone? He knew they believed more in their sinful natures than they were willing to believe in their loving ones. It just wasn't in Jesus to 'condemn', He simply COULD NOT. It wasn't in His nature to condemn for to do so would mean He would have to disconnect from GOD. Understand, now, why He prayed for the forgiveness of those who crucified Him? HIS LOVE for the Father allowed Him to only see the good in His creation even as they were behaving horribly. So where is sin, who is in sin, how does sin exist?

SIN is simply, separation from GOD. If you're connected, LOVE abounds..., disconnected, sin reigns. Your world overwhelmingly is disconnected from GOD, by choice and also by default. This also means that most of your churches are overwhelmingly disconnected from GOD. It then becomes your divine purpose as individuals to establish that reconnection to our Father, or die in that disconnection, that separation, that *sin*. Everything else you're depending on to plead your case...your good works, your continual church attendance, your living 'clean' lives, will all fail you in the end, without a true confession of faith in our FATHER and the acceptance of LOVE for all of His creation, without hesitation or doubt. End of story. This is very difficult for you, being the offspring of the Man who turned his back to GOD. But, it is not impossible to overcome, at whatever stage you become enlightened. I promise to show you the simplest way to back to GOD, but there one other attribute of GOD I must discuss first.

FORGIVENESS. If Lucifer has done a superb job of robbing you of your joy of exploration by presenting a false interpretation of the goodness of GOD, this is his crowning achievement. An unforgiving heart is at the root of all of the world's diseases. Wars, murders, rapes, domestic violence, crimes against children, property and animals are maladies that when challenged and dissected are all born out of mankind's inability or downright refusal to forgive. You live in a world that believes retribution is not only righteous but necessary for balance. This warped view of how the world should work is just another feeble attempt of mankind to *teach itself* instead of allowing the Love of GOD as manifested in the very nature and job description of the Holy Spirit to do what He's designed to do; Guide, Love and Protect.

As balanced as EDEN is, your world is its polar opposite. The labor that it takes for you to figure out for yourselves what's right, wrong, good, bad or best is energy you were never suppose to have to use in this way. Energy that would have been used to create even more goodness in your world is being diverted into maintaining some semblance of hope.

When a heart refuses to forgive, it severs the connection to that source. This means that you can no longer be your brother's keeper. Any prayers or well wishes ring hollow and become ineffective toward the change you seek, without forgiveness. This is the first lesson that Adam's sons should have taught the world and the only time it needed to be taught. Cain's inability to continue to love Abel after he received the praise for an accomplishment that Cain felt should have been his, led to the first murder. And, in that moment, there was my Loving Father, attempting to restore the balance. But Cain, like his Father, refused to take ownership for his sin (separation) and dared declare to GOD that he wasn't 'responsible' for his brother, any longer. Unrepentant and unforgiving, Cain set into motion his own plight and was driven from the presence of GOD. From that day forward, what Cain never learned or experienced was how to forgive himself for his own actions. The one who doesn't learn to forgive himself will pass along that legacy of unforgiveness and hatred. In Cain's lineage would be another murder similar in fashion to the very first, committed by his great, great grandson, Lamech. Generational legacies of hate and mistrust are ruling your world in ways that are ancient and are at the core of your existence. From our vantage point we can see that the root is never fully destroyed so most solutions are only temporary and the labor to create those solutions is simply striving in the wind, as Solomon so wisely wrote. To truly heal your land, you would have to fully turn to GOD, collectively, as a nation of people. As hard as it is for you to imagine this ever happening, I know it will, one day, *soon*. It's your only hope of salvation from your certain and complete destruction.

I promised to show you the simplest way back to GOD and this feels like the perfect time for me to do so. You've been shown it, already, but here it is in one word:

CONFESSION. What is confession? It's simply admitting what is already known to be truth. What it's not is a total absolution by nature of that confession. When Jesus was confronted with the women caught in adultery, He gave us the second and often overlooked part of confession, "Go and sin no more." Most use confession as a clean slate to just go and start again, without ever learning from those past mistakes. This is how one sin can become a generational problem. If only Adam had answered our Father, honestly, when confronted, and allowed GOD to restore his broken bond to Him, your world would have been existed in EDEN. Imagine that. Instead, I am only able to give you a small glimpse of life without fear, hate, jealousy or disease. I assure you that you can know this place of peace, too, but not because of works or deeds, but with a simple and complete surrender of desire to be anywhere but in the presence of GOD. He has to become what He has always been, the center of your universe. Everything else you've been told that should be your primary focus has only been a distraction. Sadly that's more truth than you probably can accept at this moment. However, if you're interested in going where I wish to take you, into this journey of 'what might have been', you must venture beyond this place of regret, shame and neglect, willingly.

"Blessed are the pure in Heart, for they shall see GOD."

And you thought those were just words on a page, didn't you?

Are you ready, now, to continue on the adventure of your life? My Father is calling to me. It's time, again, for one of those blessed strolls through this wonderful home and my mind will record it all, in detail, to share with you. It's my plan to ask my Father for permission in your name to show you what has never been seen. While I'm away, take this moment to review what I've told you about GOD in preparation for the remainder of this journey.

...walking with GOD

"I'm always amazed that each time, I see You, here, like this, with me ...it's as if I'm seeing You for the first time."

As much I should be prepared for this moment when I come into His Presence, especially considering the countless times it's happened, I never am. And my memory of all my declarations exposes my inadequate Grace in this moment every time, without fail. If you could only see the Majesty of His Glory... but, I must try to reveal it for you. He's telling me now that I may.

Imagining that moment of vivid sunrise or sunset on earth, with the most pleasant breeze and scent of fragrant, exotic flowers, simultaneously, comes close. But it's the amplification of the experience of each of those elements in perfect balance that just might be more accurate. But that's only the external stimuli as inside your heart races and your pulse quickens which sends blood to your brain and it awakens and everything around you is instantly heightened. Then you hear the sounds of the angelic chorus that always heralds His Entrance with the music.., the MUSIC that is so full of wonder and power and is never the same voicing, arrangements or instrumentation. In this moment it's everything I can do to hold onto my senses and not succumb to the sheer weight of the Beauty I'm allowed to Behold. He is radiant from the inside, so radiant I can't distinguish features, so there's no hair, eye or skin color.., He is luminescence in its purest form, shimmering and pulsating and alive. You can instantly understand how He has created all things because there are flashes of all that's beautiful in His Being. All of this registers in an instant, as I say to Him that I see Him for the first time, *every* time.

"Father, I am honored to be in Your Presence. You alone are Holy. I live to serve You. I Love You with all my Being."

If only I could just remember to say all this, first. It's not for a lack of trying as I've promised myself each time, to 'start with the Praise', but here I am again, doing what I always do. I feel so childlike in His Presence.

"Father."

I'm learning, finally. This used to be the moment in my excitement that I would blurt out some useless question, or attempt to seek His approval in some unnecessary manner. Today, I understand that being here, now, is all I need.

The walk has begun. I should tell you, that He doesn't 'speak' as you might, when you're strolling with a friend. His Voice, creates and when He uses it, it's always to command something into being. Our strolls are filled with impressions of His Will for me. In connection to Him, He guides our conversation with a thought. Very much in the same manner He allows The Spirit to guide you, His method with me is similar, but all the more intense because He's *right here*.

Our journey today is sort of overview of our time together. No doubt He's allowing me to see not only that He's pleased that I'm writing, but He's assisting me in understanding all that still needs to be shared. My Loving Father is always aware of my needs before I can even ask or think of them. All of EDEN is designed to please me and when I'm at one in EDEN, it pleases my Father. So here He is, again, showing me the depth of His Concern for me and my well being.

"Father, I have wanted to reveal to them everything I know, but so much of what I know, is sad."

He's telling me that nothing necessary for the greater Good can ever remain sad. Mourning always turns to Joy when the pain subsides. I know that I must record the painful truths, now, to completely reveal the Joy that He has in store for Adam's seed after they've endured the trials that are yet to come.

"Father, I desire to do all that I am designed to do, to assist your kingdom of Heaven on earth, when You are ready."

He hears nothing new in this statement as I eventually say it on every stroll. But today, I spoke it in a manner that felt different to me and He stopped walking.

We're standing here in a new vista and I'm seeing more of the color red than I would normally see on our strolls. There's always an element of balance in His creations so that no one color dominates the landscape, but here, today, I'm seeing a hint of red in everything. Suddenly, I understand why we've stopped walking.

"This is the future, isn't it?"

This is the first and only question I will ask of my Father, today.

There's an adage in your earthly vernacular that says, 'be careful what you wish for' and I can only wish I had remembered it on this stroll. I desire so much to be of complete service to my Father that I often forget that the full purpose for which I was created, is still a mystery. I wasn't just a replacement of Adam in garden, in as much as I did come into being to restore the balance of EDEN, once he departed. I am distinguished by the mere fact that I am living the life that he never got to live by simply being in the garden all this time, with GOD. I have the full call upon my life that Adam never received because of His inability to remain focused on GOD singularly. My full and distinct divine purpose is not recorded or discussed in any version of your bible, because only GOD as known it.., *'till now*.

In my desire to please my Father more, He is revealing to me, in this moment, what He has never shared before. The impressions are coming to me so rapidly, I cannot pause to consider, question or discuss them, I can only allow them to wash over me is this urgent wave of divine knowledge. As I'm illumined and enlightened, there's also a longing in my heart that's being fulfilled as I listen more deeply than ever to my Father's Will for me. The questions I never dared ask are being answered more completely than I deserve. There's a bond being created in Us by this knowledge that brings Me closer to the perfection of the Trinity than I ever desired, or believed possible.

When He finally ceases to share with me, He is gone, in an instant and EDEN is illumined more brightly than ever.

In the wake of His departure, I know who I am, *finally*, and more importantly, I know *why I am here*.

...revelation in EDEN

There is always newness in EDEN.

Not just in the creations of the vistas, but there's Joy and Wonder that lingers long after GOD has visited the garden. As I interact with the heavenly hosts and angels, I marveled at their simple, direct communication with one another and how powerful they are because of their unwavering Love and Connection to the Throne of Heaven. I never fully shared their bond, *until now*. I've just experienced something truly for the first time in EDEN.

SILENCE... In all the Heavens.

As GOD revealed my divine purpose, all of Creation stood still. This has happened only once before and that was the moment just before Jesus was born as man. It's impossible for me to describe adequately how it felt. Silence. The wind faltered, the birds perched perfectly still, not one blade of grass swayed because GOD fully focused on *Me*. It humbled me to my very core. Remember, I was created from the dust of EDEN and still GOD focused all His attention on *Me*.

I saw in a flash that every living thing that exists was named by my predecessor. There's nothing in existence that was not seen and named by the first Man. Every new discovery that someone in your earth has laid claim to, passed through EDEN, in the beginning. Solomon, the wisest man that ever lived, told you that there was nothing new under the Sun, and he was correct..., *until now*.

I always felt a connection to Apostle John, I remember how I felt in his presence, when he visited us and God showed him the future of the world and gave him that vision to record. I knew by instinct that I was being given that introduction of sorts, for a reason that was never fully revealed..., *until now*.

Apostle John recorded in Revelation 21:
> "Then I saw a new heaven and a new earth; for the first heaven and the first earth passed away..."

It was revealed to me that this home, the place I've always been, this garden of incredible Beauty and Wonder and Joy, is *the new earth* of John's Revelation. My strolls with GOD throughout the ages, were giving me a front row seat to His creation of this new earth, right here in EDEN. And now, the final revelation of my central role in all of this creation, the role I was designed to perform that my predecessor did so very well, will soon become necessary, again.

GOD is going to fully and utterly destroy mankind and its world and He's going to create it All, again.

I will be there, in that new beginning, to perform the divine task of my creation.

Everything created by GOD in EDEN, the new earth,

I will name.

I was told that the time of this re-creation is soon, so I must write with urgency. To prepare the hearts of those that will be saved and encourage those unbelievers that are destined for destruction. My simple task of recording my observations suddenly carries the weight of the world in each stroke. How will these words get to the souls that need to know them? If I could have steadied myself in His Presence during the revelation, I might have asked.., but, just as the Angels that serve Him without hesitation, I understand that especially now, *so must I*. There are no more questions I ever need ask of my Father. I understand the gravity of His Love for His original creation and realize now that He has already answered me when He told me during our stroll that 'mourning always turns to Joy when the pain subsides'.

Therefore, I must write to help as many as I can, for my Father's sake.

...beyond EDEN

I have lived in EDEN all my life, which by your standard of measure is your complete world's history. I saw the struggles of Adam and Eve, the plight of their offspring, the corruption that came quickly upon that seed as they allowed their daughters to couple with the 'sons of GOD' and I saw the fallen angels referred to in Genesis 6 as Nephilim walk the earth in obvious contempt of God. You thought Adam was truly alone, save his family, didn't you? But have you ever wondered how God's creation could fall so quickly after leaving the garden that it begged their destruction? The answer comes from the scripture that you consider to be your Holy Bible, although no one has ever adequately interpreted these passages. But did you know that there was an even deeper revelation of this period of time that was deleted from your sacred texts? Let's look deeper into that time and illumine what happened, after Adam left EDEN, as recorded in Genesis 6: The verses that few understand and most ignore entirely.

Genesis 6:

1. Now it came about, when men began to multiply on the face of the land, and daughters were born to them.

2. that the sons of God saw that the daughters of men were beautiful; and they took wives for themselves, whomever they chose.

3. Then the LORD said, "My Spirit shall not strive with man forever, because he also is flesh; nevertheless his days shall be one hundred and twenty years."

4. The Nephilim were on the earth in those days, and also afterward, when the sons of God came in to the

daughters of men, and they bore children to them. Those were the mighty men who were of old, men of renown.

5. Then the LORD saw that the wickedness of man was great on the earth, and that every intent of the thoughts of his heart was only evil continually.

6. The LORD was sorry that He had made man on the earth, and He was grieved in His heart.

7. The LORD said, "I will blot out man whom I have created from the face of the land, from man to animals to creeping things and to birds of the sky; for I am sorry that I have made them."

8. But Noah found favor in the eyes of the LORD.

So much that should have been told you, to keep you from the same destruction of the first generation of Adam's offspring, was hidden away from you in similar passages as this because, as I've written prior, there are those who guard the truth because they have always been afraid of ultimate power. This is also why most learned men reject the Bible because they are painfully aware that they're not getting the whole story. Question the veracity of the Bible and you're led to believe that you're having a crisis of faith for daring to question those passages that lack understanding and clarification. But, aren't you truly attempting to increase your faith, by understanding? These gatekeepers will soon know the full wrath of GOD for the evil they have done under the sun.

When Adam walked out of EDEN, he walked into an *inhabited* world. A world populated by Nephilim and other fallen creatures, sometimes referred to as Watchers, and they were poised and positioned to become nemesis to Adam and his offspring. At that time, EDEN was still connected to the world at large and others could come and go from it as evidenced by Lucifer's presence. As long was Adam was connected to God, these entities were not only invisible to him, but their influence was ineffective. That remained true, until the failure of Adam to resist the advances of Eve. Once that transpired, they could not remain in EDEN, or the corruption would have spread throughout.

Lucifer was not alone when he departed Heaven for his new home. John in Revelations 12 reveals the battle that led to his departure which caused a third of the angelic hosts to fall with him. The question for many has always been the timetable of this battle and an even deeper question is when did he take dominion of the world outside EDEN? These answers are addressed by John as well in that same chapter, which I'll share later. But the simple answer, for now, is indeed, he was there *before* Adam was created.

If only you were allowed to read the Book of Enoch as part of your original biblical education, none of my writing, now, would be necessary. So much that he was shown by GOD eclipsed John's Revelation and had his visions remained part of your Holy Scriptures, there would have been no need for any further Revelation. If you need to understand the importance of Enoch, again look no further than your acceptable texts.

Genesis 5: 21. Enoch lived sixty-five years, and became the father of Methuselah. 22. Then Enoch walked with God three hundred years after he became the father of Methuselah, and he had others sons and daughters. 23. So all the days of Enoch were three hundred and sixty-five years. **24. Enoch walked with God; and he was not, for God took him.**

There have only been three men in your world's history that have been allowed to 'escape' death by simply being taken into the presence of GOD. You know of Elijah and Moses.., but few remember the first was *Enoch*. For you, his story ends, there. But it was far from over, indeed, it had truly just begun. Once he was caught up into heaven, he became an ambassador of sorts between the fallen angels, the Watchers and GOD and was uniquely positioned to restore the world back into balance had his words not only been heeded at that time and allowed to complete their divine purpose, in harmony with the rest of scripture. All through your Bible are references to his texts, without the full accounting of them, by the prophets and Jesus. His accounts of this time before the flood is illumination personified. Here in the opening chapter, he gave us an overview of the time of his departure as well as glimpse into our certain future.

The Book of Enoch; Chapter 1

1 The words of the blessing of Enoch, wherewith he blessed the elect and righteous, who will be
2 living in the day of tribulation, when all the wicked and godless are to be removed. And he took up his parable and said -Enoch a righteous man, whose eyes were opened by God, saw the vision of the Holy One in the heavens, which the angels showed me, and from

them I heard everything, and from them I understood as I saw, but not for this generation, but for a remote one which is for to come.

3 Concerning the elect I said, and took up my parable concerning them:

The Holy Great One will come forth from His dwelling,
4 And the eternal God will tread upon the earth, (even) on Mount Sinai,
[And appear from His camp]
And appear in the strength of His might from the heaven of heavens.

5 And all shall be smitten with fear
And the Watchers shall quake,
And great fear and trembling shall seize them unto the ends of the earth.

6 And the high mountains shall be shaken,
And the high hills shall be made low,
And shall melt like wax before the flame

7 And the earth shall be wholly rent in sunder,
And all that is upon the earth shall perish,
And there shall be a judgment upon all (men).

8 But with the righteous He will make peace.

And will protect the elect,
And mercy shall be upon them.

And they shall all belong to God,
And they shall be prospered,
And they shall all be blessed.

And He will help them all,
And light shall appear unto them,
And He will make peace with them'.

9 And behold! He cometh with ten thousands of His holy ones

To execute judgment upon all,
And to destroy all the ungodly:

And to convict all flesh
Of all the works of their ungodliness which they have
ungodly committed,
And of all the hard things which ungodly sinners have
spoken against Him.

To question Enoch's veracity is to also question John in Revelation, as he reveals even more depth to the truth recorded by Enoch. The 12th chapter is an overview of the first battle waged in Heaven with Lucifer, then called The Red Dragon, Satan and in that battle according to his 4th verse, a third of the stars (angels) of Heaven fell to earth with him. So the corruption we see in Genesis 6 is intensified by the presence of these fallen angelic beings that were poised and positioned to take advantage of Adam's offspring. Becoming a hindrance to the seed of Adam in the earth would become their earthly mission played out through the ages.

Revelations 12

[1] Then I witnessed in heaven an event of great significance. I saw a woman clothed with the sun, with the moon beneath her feet, and a crown of twelve stars on her head. [2] She was pregnant, and she cried out because of her labor pains and the agony of giving birth.

[3] Then I witnessed in heaven another significant event. I saw a large red dragon with seven heads and

ten horns, with seven crowns on his heads. 4 His tail swept away one-third of the stars in the sky, and he threw them to the earth. He stood in front of the woman as she was about to give birth, ready to devour her baby as soon as it was born.

5 She gave birth to a son who was to rule all nations with an iron rod. And her child was snatched away from the dragon and was caught up to God and to his throne. 6 And the woman fled into the wilderness, where God had prepared a place to care for her for 1,260 days.

7 Then there was war in heaven. Michael and his angels fought against the dragon and his angels. 8 And the dragon lost the battle, and he and his angels were forced out of heaven. 9 This great dragon—the ancient serpent called the devil, or Satan, the one deceiving the whole world—was thrown down to the earth with all his angels.

10 Then I heard a loud voice shouting across the heavens,

"It has come at last—
    salvation and power
and the Kingdom of our God,
    and the authority of his Christ.
For the accuser of our brothers and sisters
    has been thrown down to earth—
the one who accuses them
    before our God day and night.
11 And they have defeated him by the blood of the Lamb
    and by their testimony.
And they did not love their lives so much
    that they were afraid to die.
12 Therefore, rejoice, O heavens!
    And you, who live in the heavens, rejoice!

But terror will come on the earth and the sea,
  for the devil has come down to you in great anger,
    knowing that he has little time.”

¹³ When the dragon realized that he had been thrown down to the earth, he pursued the woman who had given birth to the male child. ¹⁴ But she was given two wings like those of a great eagle so she could fly to the place prepared for her in the wilderness. There she would be cared for and protected from the dragon for a time, times, and half a time.

¹⁵ Then the dragon tried to drown the woman with a flood of water that flowed from his mouth. ¹⁶ But the earth helped her by opening its mouth and swallowing the river that gushed out from the mouth of the dragon. ¹⁷ And the dragon was angry at the woman and declared war against the rest of her children—all who keep God's commandments and maintain their testimony for Jesus.

¹⁸ Then the dragon took his stand on the shore beside the sea.

Let's you become confused, allow me to illumine that 'the woman' spoken of in verses 13-17 is not a reference to Mary and the birth of Jesus, as many have preached, but the reference here is your home, *mother earth*, as it's commonly known by those that see earth as living being. In that reference, the male child is Adam, and Lucifer witnessing this birth/creation was instantly threatened knowing that his dominion on earth was about to challenged. When he failed to achieve his true goal, the subjugation of EDEN, he turned his attention on the created man and waged battle for dominion of his mind, envying his ability of choice and decision, attributes he never fully possessed, without inhabitation of another. It was this moment, as referenced in verse 14, that GOD caused EDEN, the womb of mother earth, to be hidden from all of those but the pure in heart. Please review Revelation 12 with this illumination in mind.

Knowing the presence of this inherent evil, my Loving Father provided protection for a season for Adam and his offspring, beyond the departure from EDEN. But, He soon grew despondent over their continual evil choices and only then did he decide to destroy the entire world to rid himself of it and all its inhabited evil. Had he not found Noah who is introduced at the end of Genesis 6, a good man to save, all the world would have ended as quickly as it had begun. Choosing Noah to continue meant my Father didn't have to create the whole population of earth, again. As the story is told, Noah was given the plans to build the Ark directly from GOD to save his family and all the animal life. The details of all this is recorded in the 7th and 8th chapters of Genesis.

I will pause to share your recorded version of Noah and the flood now, as a reference for you for what's to come, because there's so much more to glean from these passages as you're about to experience for yourself.

Genesis 6

⁸ But Noah found favor with the Lord.

The Story of Noah

⁹ This is the account of Noah and his family. Noah was a righteous man, the only blameless person living on earth at the time, and he walked in close fellowship with God. ¹⁰ Noah was the father of three sons: Shem, Ham, and Japheth.

¹¹ Now God saw that the earth had become corrupt and was filled with violence. ¹² God observed all this corruption in the world, for everyone on earth was corrupt. ¹³ So God said to Noah, "I have decided to destroy all living creatures, for they have filled the earth with violence. Yes, I will wipe them all out along with the earth!

¹⁴ "Build a large boat from cypress wood and waterproof it with tar, inside and out. Then construct decks and stalls throughout its interior. ¹⁵ Make the boat 450 feet long, 75 feet wide, and 45 feet high. ¹⁶ Leave an 18-inch opening below the roof all the way around the boat. Put the door on the side, and build three decks inside the boat—lower, middle, and upper.

¹⁷ "Look! I am about to cover the earth with a flood that will destroy every living thing that breathes. Everything on earth will die. ¹⁸ But I will confirm my covenant with you. So enter the boat—you and your wife and your sons and their wives. ¹⁹ Bring a pair of every kind of animal—a male and a female—into the boat with you to keep them alive during the flood.

²⁰ Pairs of every kind of bird, and every kind of animal, and every kind of small animal that scurries along the ground, will come to you to be kept alive. ²¹ And be sure

to take on board enough food for your family and for all the animals."

²² So Noah did everything exactly as God had commanded him.

Genesis 7

The Flood Covers the Earth

¹ When everything was ready, the Lord said to Noah, "Go into the boat with all your family, for among all the people of the earth, I can see that you alone are righteous. ² Take with you seven pairs—male and female—of each animal I have approved for eating and for sacrifice, and take one pair of each of the others. ³ Also take seven pairs of every kind of bird. There must be a male and a female in each pair to ensure that all life will survive on the earth after the flood. ⁴ Seven days from now I will make the rains pour down on the earth. And it will rain for forty days and forty nights, until I have wiped from the earth all the living things I have created."

⁵ So Noah did everything as the Lord commanded him.

⁶ Noah was 600 years old when the flood covered the earth.

⁷ He went on board the boat to escape the flood—he and his wife and his sons and their wives. ⁸ With them were all the various kinds of animals—those approved for eating and for sacrifice and those that were not—along with all the birds and the small animals that scurry along the ground. ⁹ They entered the boat in

pairs, male and female, just as God had commanded Noah. ¹⁰ After seven days, the waters of the flood came and covered the earth.

¹¹ When Noah was 600 years old, on the seventeenth day of the second month, all the underground waters erupted from the earth, and the rain fell in mighty torrents from the sky. ¹² The rain continued to fall for forty days and forty nights.

¹³ That very day Noah had gone into the boat with his wife and his sons—Shem, Ham, and Japheth—and their wives. ¹⁴ With them in the boat were pairs of every kind of animal—domestic and wild, large and small—along with birds of every kind. ¹⁵ Two by two they came into the boat, representing every living thing that breathes. ¹⁶ A male and female of each kind entered, just as God had commanded Noah. Then the Lord closed the door behind them.

¹⁷ For forty days the floodwaters grew deeper, covering the ground and lifting the boat high above the earth. ¹⁸ As the waters rose higher and higher above the ground, the boat floated safely on the surface. ¹⁹ Finally, the water covered even the highest mountains on the earth, ²⁰ rising more than twenty-two feet above the highest peaks. ²¹ All the living things on earth died—birds, domestic animals, wild animals, small animals that scurry along the ground, and all the people. ²² Everything that breathed and lived on dry land died. ²³ God wiped out every living thing on the earth—people, livestock, small animals that scurry along the ground, and the birds of the sky. All were destroyed. The only people who survived were Noah and those with him in the boat. ²⁴ And the floodwaters covered the earth for 150 days.

Genesis 8

The Flood Recedes

¹ But God remembered Noah and all the wild animals and livestock with him in the boat. He sent a wind to blow across the earth, and the floodwaters began to recede. ² The underground waters stopped flowing, and the torrential rains from the sky were stopped. ³ So the floodwaters gradually receded from the earth. After 150 days, ⁴ exactly five months from the time the flood began, the boat came to rest on the mountains of Ararat.

⁵ Two and a half months later, as the waters continued to go down, other mountain peaks became visible.

⁶ After another forty days, Noah opened the window he had made in the boat ⁷ and released a raven. The bird flew back and forth until the floodwaters on the earth had dried up. ⁸ He also released a dove to see if the water had receded and it could find dry ground. ⁹ But the dove could find no place to land because the water still covered the ground. So it returned to the boat, and Noah held out his hand and drew the dove back inside. ¹⁰ After waiting another seven days, Noah released the dove again. ¹¹ This time the dove returned to him in the evening with a fresh olive leaf in its beak. Then Noah knew that the floodwaters were almost gone. ¹² He waited another seven days and then released the dove again. This time it did not come back.

¹³ Noah was now 601 years old. On the first day of the new year, ten and a half months after the flood began, the floodwaters had almost dried up from the earth. Noah lifted back the covering of the boat and saw that the surface of the ground was drying. ¹⁴ Two more months went by, and at last the earth was dry!

¹⁵ Then God said to Noah, ¹⁶ "Leave the boat, all of you—you and your wife, and your sons and their wives. ¹⁷ Release all the animals—the birds, the livestock, and the small animals that scurry along the ground—so they can be fruitful and multiply throughout the earth."

¹⁸ So Noah, his wife, and his sons and their wives left the boat. ¹⁹ And all of the large and small animals and birds came out of the boat, pair by pair.

²⁰ Then Noah built an altar to the Lord, and there he sacrificed as burnt offerings the animals and birds that had been approved for that purpose. ²¹ And the Lord was pleased with the aroma of the sacrifice and said to himself, "I will never again curse the ground because of the human race, even though everything they think or imagine is bent toward evil from childhood. I will never again destroy all living things. ²² As long as the earth remains, there will be planting and harvest, cold and heat, summer and winter, day and night."

I promise you, right here and now, I am not sharing with you all this knowledge to destroy your Faith, but to build it up and have it fortified for a firmer foundation for what's to be revealed. All I wish to highlight especially from the story of Noah is that GOD has not come to His present day decision to utterly destroy your world, lightly. In fact, this account of Noah's, I must also tell you, isn't the first and only accounting of a flood destroying mankind. All your faiths know of a central GOD with the same attributes, but Satan and his minions have done an incredible job of conquering and dividing the faithful among to keep you weak and ineffective and ultimately 'no real threat to themselves'. You've finally come to a time and place in your history that GOD must do whatever He must to preserve and promote Holiness in your world. What has made this moment so startling is He has revealed that to truly be rid of evil in your world, there must be a full destruction of those that have corrupted His Truth.

What God finally revealed to me, is that in order to have a people worthy of EDEN, the new earth, there can be no connection to the original Adam. Man must be *created again*, in accordance with His original design. However, before I can begin to discuss that future event, I owe you an accounting from my own unique perspective of just how profoundly you've gone off course, when left to your imaginings and creative impulses beyond God's presence. Even beyond the flood, when everything was 'new again', just look at how the descendants of Noah behaved not very long after being spared from the destruction of the world.

...after the FLOOD

Undoubtedly, man has a natural propensity to evil. The best evidence of this is immediately after the flood that destroyed the wickedness that roamed the earth. Shortly after Noah's death, having lived for nine hundred and fifty years, the world had become populated through the offspring of his three sons and the generations that followed.

Genesis 11:

1 Now the whole earth used the same language and the same words. 2 It came about as they journeyed east, that they found a plain in the land of Shinar and settled there. 3 They said to one another, "Come, let us make bricks and burn *them* thoroughly." And they used brick for stone, and they used tar for mortar. 4 They said, "Come, let us build for ourselves a city, and a tower whose top *will reach* into heaven, and let us make for ourselves a name, otherwise we will be scattered abroad over the face of the whole earth." 5 The LORD came down to see the city and the tower which the sons of men had built. 6 The LORD said, "Behold, they are one people, and they all have the same language. And this is what they began to do, and now nothing which they purpose to do will be impossible for them. 7 "Come, let Us go down and there confuse their language, so that they will not understand one another's speech." 8 So the LORD scattered them abroad from there over the face of the whole earth; and they stopped building the city. 9 Therefore its name was called Babel, because there the LORD confused the language of the whole earth; and from there the LORD scattered them abroad over the face of the whole earth.

This history of man to always choose wrongly when given opportunities for new beginnings could never be allowed to enter EDEN, the new earth. Hiding EDEN away from the destruction of the world was only the first part of GOD's prophetic plan. This present day failure of the inhabitants of your world to continually choose evil over Good, and the rejection of the only bridge between darkness and Light, namely Jesus, leaves GOD with only one choice. GOD sees this restoration to his original design as necessary because of the choices man continues to make with his free will. When the destruction finally begins, no one will be more saddened than GOD at the lost of souls and the equal lost of their unbridled creative energy. Man has exhibited little or no regard for the real desires of my Father or His Will for them. It is ultimately for this 'sin' alone, they will pay with the death of all that they call their own.

Forgive me for having to be so technical, but in order for your minds to be unleashed to see the vision I have to share with you, it was important that I attempt to lay a proper foundation for these truths. Without this basic knowledge the weight of my words would surely cause a collapse of heart and will to receive all that must be shared. This world that you call your home is everything that was created beyond the flood. This is your final chance to see the goodness in yourself and others, before GOD has to end it all. While there is still time to save you, I must do what Noah did, without a physical ark. I'm being allowed to create a safe place for you, constructed of words, an ark of understanding that will not only protect your souls, but gather your creative energies into unified harmony and it's that much sought after gift of collective reasoning that's your most valued resource to GOD and the enemy of your peace. In all the time of your earthly existence, man has only been connected, once, as recorded in Genesis 11 and instead of being reason and Light to the world, those minds only wanted to be gods. Instinctual by nature, they knew they were capable of great things, but squandered their talents in a feeble attempt to make a 'name' for themselves. When I look at all the resources you've wasted building monuments to dead heroes and dead works, I'm saddened, knowing the full intention of your creative minds have never completely grasped their unlimited power. There were Nubian prophets, Egyptians scholars and both had architects that rival the best of your best *2000 years* before the birth of Christ and that knowledge had to be scattered because you only wanted a 'name' for yourselves and failed to honor or recognize the GOD of all creation. That wealth of knowledge is still available to you. Dormant and disconnected because of war and greed, but I write now as a clarion call to awaken all the sleeping intellectual, spiritual and mystical giants. Those who have known all this time their gifts were being underused and abused and who have secretly suspected that were being 'saved' for a special time and place. It's time to awaken those genetically predisposed and chosen for the cataclysmic events necessary to usher change into your world. This is that time and place for those of you who believe you are chosen for this moment of new birth. It's time to create that safe haven for the scattered brethren throughout the lands of your dying earth. It's time to awaken all those dormant souls and birth them into one consciousness, one thought and purpose and to allow them to feel the comfort in knowing that they are not alone, and reverse the curse of Babel.

This is that moment.

It's time to wake up.

...the Awakening

Suddenly, there was a SOUND.

Like that of a mighty rushing wind – but more finely tuned. Steady streams of rushing air – an audible hissing throughout the heavens. The Sound's moving, rushing headlong, and filling the void with intention and purpose. Inside that Sound is life, pulsating, palpable – distinct ...and *ancient*. Not sinister, but just as determined – focused. Yes, the Sounds have purpose – in their wings. I know this Sound.

It's the Sound of Flight.

It's Begun!

BOOK TWO
Prologue

But how could that be?

Out there, beyond earth's atmosphere – and how could I know
that Sound ...*Remember* that Sound? That rushing river of
wind and intention – that driven, pin-focused energy is
moving *directly for me*.

How could I hear;
How could I know;
What could I do, but

"WAKE UP !!"

"WAKE UP !!"

Is that my thought? How is it so loud in my own head? No,
that is not my voice – but it's familiar.

"WAKE UP !!"

Is it repeating itself – or is the sound reaching into the recesses of my brain – deeper into my mind than I ever knew sound could travel – something, in me, not me, but always a part of me, is responding against my will, perhaps, *but with my consent* – responding to the command as a soldier would to his General – immediate without hesitation. An awakened dormant part in me, alert and now responsive, was reaching out to greet The Voice and Sound with strange familiarity.

Finally, reunited, conjoined and connected, again.

What is this??

What's happening to me?

I awoke, drenched in sweat, sensitive to the morning light – and if I didn't recall that I was three years sober, I might have assumed I was nursing a hangover.

But I did remember.

More than a dream, my body felt the effects only an abrupt exertion, a surge of adrenaline can produce – something was present I had not sensed before. I felt strangely 'alive' and it was that heightened awareness that caused the morning light to be more intense than in recent memory – if ever.

As I walked past the vanity, thinking only of the warm water awaiting me in the my shower, I caught a glimpse of someone I hadn't seen in more than a few years – I was looking at a man I hadn't been for some time, now. *Overnight*, I seemed to have aged, *in reverse!* The body staring back at me belonged to me, yes, but the me of '19' – not that I'd let myself go totally at 26 – but my recent troubles had not allowed me to exercise as I once did. Before that, the college drinking, poor diet and late night studying of med school had begun to exact a physical toil. The man reflected back to me now was only in my memory, *'till now.*

Standing in that stream of hot liquid, I was washing away more than the night sweats. It felt as if the man I had been, all the mornings before now, was disappearing as quickly as the water circling the drain. Emerging naked into my bedroom, I had the sense of an open window on a wintry day – except it was the month of July. With no thought to my exposure, I stepped out onto the terrace, into my back yard – needing instinctively to bathe my body in the sun, to feel my feet in the warm grass. The rays of Light struck me like a bolt – and coursed through my whole being charging me from within. No, this wasn't mere arousal, it was electric – a current that stimulated my muscles, every muscle save my maleness, which remained totally unaffected. Whatever this was, the signal wasn't centered in my brain.., but the origin seemed to be the Sun itself – not just my imagination.

Stepping quickly back indoors, I felt an immediate lessening in intensity, but still a presence that led me to reach out to hold onto something as my body started to convulse – my back bending making me fall to by knees as I might in prayer. The heat beneath my skin shifted and centered in my back, where my shoulder blades burned without pain.

Then, I heard it again – the sound from the earlier dream. That same pulsating, rushing sound but this time, not in my dreams.., nor at a distance, but totally present.., near – 'till I realized that I was creating that displacement of wind and space – that pulsating was coming *from me,* by newly formed WINGS – extending from my searing back, just beneath my shoulders.

Everything in my room was disturbed, especially my bed which was swept back with the gentle force of a tempest wind – without thought I turned back in the direction of my terrace – an shot out in the morning air again, but this time my feet never touched a single blade of grass. As I soared out into the expanse, faster than humanly perceptible, I had a sense that I wasn't alone. When I ceased to move, but hovered just beyond the first barrier of clouds, I saw the others as they equally acknowledged my presence.
Startling, each hanging above his country of origin – beautiful and magnificent, poised as if for battle – now activated, awaiting, anticipating...

That Sound from my dreams was now tangible, present and Real.

"It's TIME."

...Three Year Journey of Awakening

"Why did I have that last shot?"

I knew how important this day would be – that I not only needed to focus – but I needed a steady hand as I sterilized for my final surgical exam. Thank Goodness I didn't go into heart surgery, as originally planned as now, a possible botched nose job doesn't quite fall into the category of life or death. Well, certainly not physically but a case could be made I suppose, socially. I would just have to make my incisions slow and deliberate, praying to appear more like an artist, than an unskilled plastic surgeon student.

It wasn't the last shot that compromised me – it was the last year in totality. Slowly losing interest in everything I once held dear or at least important allowed my judgment to become questionable. Losing focus wasn't the worse of it, nor the alcohol, it was losing 'the vision'.., the one that I'd held of my life for as long as I could remember. Feeling distressed over the need to create something greater than sculpting perfect noses, was becoming lost in the over-whelming and ever mounting debt of school. Whatever that vision had been, was being co-opted by the 'real world' I was quickly finding myself totally focused upon.

At least I hadn't had the dreams, now, in over a year.., hadn't heard The Voice even longer. Did I ever – or was it just my over-stimulated imagination as I'd been told so often by so many? Whatever had been prohibiting those visions wasn't being helped by the addition of the alcohol, no doubt. I just needed to finish this last exam without incident, so I can take that cushy job awaiting me in B to the E to the V *Hills*. Yeah, I know I've sold out as the cliché goes, but what's a boy to do, especially one with such expectations and obligations? (I'm sure my taste in expensive cars might weigh just a little into my decision.) I'm not shallow, so don't get the wrong idea.., but I am very tired of swimming against the tide and believing in that childish fantasy that I was *chosen* and destined for greater things. Why did I ever believe that prophecy? Maybe because it seemed to validate the dreams, echo The Voice that told me that *and more*... 'till I drowned it out with the pressures of school – the booze.., and the beautiful, never ending study partners that became more about the sleepover than the study sessions.

No matter – this is my reality, now and I suppose, all told, there could be worst fates. Anyway, my next two years will be set. All I have to do is get through these next hours of final exam without incident. I can do this procedure in my sleep, which is a good thing, 'because I never got to bed last night. Well, let's just say, I never got around to sleeping.

Three Hours Later…

I swear I don't know how I found it... What made me order that second set of X-Rays? What's even more disturbing is that this isn't the first time I've sensed 'destiny' intervening at a critical moment. That little smudge was nearly imperceptible and had I made that first incision, without seeing it – no doubt she would have bled out on the table. A simple nose job had revealed a trace of even larger cancerous tumor and this surgical student not only found it, but assisted in its immediate biopsy and sequentially made his reputation before even stitching her up. Yes, its official – Someone is watching over me! But, all I can care about now is that I need to sleep something fierce. And for the first time in a long while – I need it to be alone.

Most definitely, *Alone*.

...into the LIGHT

I would like to think it all a dream – but it was more real than that. All I can recall was I was so tired, I didn't even remove my sneakers. I just collapsed on my bed, sprawled out like I anticipated being crucified before dawn. When I awoke, still in the thick of night, I thought somehow a cruel joke was being played on me... Who knew that the darkness that enveloped me was the result of a rolling brownout?? It was enough of a jolt to my senses to be so clothe in darkness and sleep-deprived on top of it all, that I called out a name in that thick ink that I hadn't said intentionally in my twenties.

"Jesus Christ !!" is all I remember saying before being pierced with a shaft of Light that seemed to penetrate the bedroom ceiling straight from the heavens. As if that wasn't startling enough, The Voice that responded, "YES", moved me from disorientation to fear instantly. Silent and trembling, I waited for the illusion to pass – only to have the voice to now call me by name...

"Yes, Dathan, I am here."

Did I faint, or fall back to sleep – or was I ever awake, I can't be certain, but when I awoke again, to what appeared to be a normal day, with all the news discussing the freakish black out, I felt strangely dissuaded that 'though they might be able to explain my vision of darkness, there was nothing being reported that could explain The Voice I'd heard, again. Yes, *again*. It wasn't the first time I'd been singled out, but this time my mother wasn't there to explain it all away as my 'fever' breaking or as nightmares from too much TV. No sleepovers this time unexpectedly awakened by my sudden outbursts to tell me I ate something that didn't agree me. This time I knew that the voice was demanding I pay attention once and for all. I would like to say I heard it and obeyed, but in fact, ...I would go back into the clinic later that day to be regaled as the Midas doctor with the divine eyes to match his miraculous hands and I believed them, naturally. It would be a couple of more years before The Voice would call out to me again and that time, I could no longer ignore it.., or its message.

...into the NIGHT

Driving home from that AA Meeting, still palming my two year pen, I knew I should feel good about the accomplishment, but I couldn't shake the feeling that this was only the beginning of something much deeper; That being sober was necessary – but not everything. I was lost in thought and never saw the stalled car in the middle of the road. When I did, all I could do was turn hard, causing me to not only lose control, but to flip three times the on-lookers would report. No injuries to the stalled car inhabits (a miracle) but with me in a coma, it was speculated my career as a plastic surgeon was over or certainly compromised as I would undoubtedly have some brain damaged, if and when I awoke. In that nebulous place, The Voice came to visit again and this time I had to listen, and It had much to say. Years of preparation was being condensed in each syllable as I listened with silent tears streaming down my still cheeks. I was a finally a willing pupil and a captive audience.

Being shown your life, the foolish mistakes, the folly and the fear, is not an exercise I would wish upon anyone, who isn't prepared.., or *chosen*. In retrospect, I had almost asked for something this dramatic to happen, failing to pause at all the attempts to capture my attention prior to the accident. Besides the usual 'This is Your Life' fare, I was being given a glimpse into something more that should have encouraged me – instead it seemed more implausible than ever that the life I was being shown could ever be my own. I simply just didn't feel worthy after years of abuse and neglect. How could I still be used in the manner I was being shown? Awaking to months of rehabilitation, I had to gradually accept that only what 'might have been' could possibly be the outcome of my latest vision. The Voice had simply gotten it wrong.

I awoke also to find myself without my career, being able only to consult, while no longer being capable of performing lengthy surgeries, due to uncontrollable bouts of dizziness. The only ray of light was that in spite of these setbacks and disappointments, I actually was in a good place emotionally. So much so, I never considered drinking, or my partaking of my usual diet of sleepovers, to comfort me. Instead, I read – searching for others who've heard voices (The Voice), seen the Light or just survived near death. In the search, I found GOD, not just personally (He was always there), but more so *collectively* weaving throughout all the experiences that I researched. Called by different names, but celebrated much the same, He was given credit as the reason for the recoveries, the healings, the visions.., the mystery of our uniqueness..., *all GOD*. I also recognized something else in the accounts, a commonality that might have gone unnoticed had I not been one with such an intimate knowledge of this information I sought.

When these testimonials were interviewed, I saw a certain signature in the others that seemed to mirror my own journey – which they, too, had been 'called out to' all their lives. Beaconed in the darkness by some unseen presence and all brought to a place where they had to respond by listening. Discovering that I was not alone, I began to believe that the visions were not being delayed, or denied – but determined for a specific time. I would become obsessed in my desire to not only pinpoint this future moment – but to find others who might be a part of this impending event.
In my studies, I found a word that seemed to describe us perfectly. That word was;

ATAVISM:

The term ATAVISM is employed to express the reappearance of characteristics, physical or psychical, in the individual, or in the race, which are supposed to have been possessed at one time by *remote ancestors*.
An atavism is an evolutionary throwback, such as traits reappearing which had disappeared generations ago. Atavisms occur because genes for previously existing phenotypical features are often preserved in DNA, even though the genes are not expressed in some or most of the organisms possessing them.

If we indeed were connected, by some dormant gene, with only our visions and The Voice as evidence of this connection, I could only assume that more was to come, in the time between now and that fateful event of our visions. I needed to know more. I had to meet some of my fellow sojourners and I knew now that this was exactly the best use of my time away from surgery. My life was beginning to feel ordered again. Mind you, I still had questions as to what it all meant, but for now, I had hope and excitement.., *and joy*. Something was slowly being awakened in me, I could feel it.., and I had no time to spare.

If only I could have been more prepared for what I was about to learn.

...Atavists Revealed

Ethiopia.

Africa.

I am on a flight headed to the Motherland. Honestly, of all the places I thought I would travel to, this wasn't even on the list. I saw myself in Monte Carlo, or the Bahamas.., *never Ethiopia*! But the research led me to this location overwhelmingly as a central starting point of all the commonly shared vision dreams of those that I had singled out as representing my unique dormant atavism. The oldest of this group, lives in Ethiopia, *still.* I needed to know what connected me to him and I knew instinctively, that my answers were forthcoming.

I decided to come to Ethiopia against the advice of all my friends, 'tho that number had dwindled as I'd become more and more obsessed with The Voice. Although I only had The Voice in my head as guide, I thought I would have no trouble finding a physical guide, once I landed, as there were so many locals in need of income. Underscoring this thought, when a small fight erupted when I asked to be taken to Lalibela, I mistakenly thought the ruckus was entirely due to the potential windfall of my two weeks visit. But as the guides slowly all stepped away from me, I realized that they were attempting to get a consensus from the other guides to all abandon me. I would learn later that they were all paid to keep as many foreigners out of Lalibela. Asking to go there, without introduction or invitation was akin to landing in Rome and expecting to be taken directly into Vatican City. Not only is this city protected by the locals, it's revered by them. I knew historically, that Ethiopians were a practicing Christians as early as the fourth century, when most of Europe was populated by barbarians; they made Christianity the state religion. But this reverence for the city of Lalibela was totally unexpected. The city had been built in design to model Jerusalem by its name sake, Gebre Mesqel Lalibela, who had spent his youth in that holy city. It was believed that Building the monolithic churches, known now for their rock-cut architecture, had been a labor of love and pure devotion and they were built with amazing speed. His desire to give his devoted Orthodox Christians a sacred city also meant that it had to be fiercely guarded. So much so, that the first European to ever see the legendary churches was the Portugal explorer, Pero da Covilha, in the 15th century. I had read his words with a particular interest about his experience.

> "I weary of writing more about these buildings, because it seems to me that I shall not be believed if I write more... I swear my God, in Whose power I am, that all I have written is truth."

In this moment, I felt betrayed by The Voice, believing my trip to be in vain, and I wondered if I would ever get to see this sacred city or have the rendezvous I'd been promised.

Out of the corner of my eye, I saw a young man, who had distanced himself from the crowd. His demeanor was ethereal and I was immediately drawn to him. Without speaking a word, he beckoned me to him and as I approached, the other guides fell deathly silent.

"Dathan, I thought you would never arrive."

Hearing my name, on the lips of a stranger in this strange land, immediately relaxed me, but the feeling wasn't as unusual as it might had been had I not recognized...

'The Voice'.

Standing before me, in the flesh, was The Voice I'd been hearing all this time. I never ever considered it to be 'real'. I am excited and apprehensive, reminiscence of the feeling I first had, so long ago, during my recuperation. As I drew nearer, I suddenly realized that there were only two men standing, me and the beautiful gentle man that called me by name. His appearance had caused all within view of him to fall to their knees. Who was this man? I was soon to discover that I was being introduced to much more than a guide.

I was about to granted an audience with the guardian *Angel of Lalibela.*

...Angel of Lalibela

"I am Uriel."

Before I could react to the pronouncement, he followed with a not so innocent question that felt more like a challenge.

"Perhaps you've heard of me,
if you've done your research as thoroughly as I suspect?"

Uriel! Was I to believe that The Angel that guided Enoch and Ezra of the Old Testament and was positioned at the entrance of the Garden of Eden to keep out the Watchers and the sons of men from gaining entry to the Tree of Life, was standing before me, now? The very same angel that was rumored to have buried Adam and Abel in Paradise... was standing before me and speaking to me, now.

"Uriel."

Sensing that I was at a loss for words beyond the feeble mention of his name, he spoke again.

"Dathan, *it's time.*
Soon you will join the others, but now, it is time for you to discover exactly who you are.
Come with me, *now.*"

As soon as he spoke the word *now*, we were transported from the audience of guides to the top of the Bête Golgotha, the tallest of the monolithic structures I had come to see. There, on the roof of this church that descended three stories *into the earth*, I was told that this particular structure was the actually the resting home of King Lalibela, who was given the privilege of burial near the Tomb of Adam for his faithful service in the construction of these eleven church. Legend has it that an angel took him to heaven, where God gave him the vision of churches no man had ever seen. I would learn that angel was Uriel who also assisted the King, nightly, to build these magnificent edifices. Here in this Northern Group of structures my education would begin. As far from home as I'd ever been, I felt strangely at peace as I begin to learn about my lineage and my atavism.

Uriel was patient with me, when he obviously didn't need to be. I was every bit a captive audience, not only because of our perch atop the church, but mostly because I was enraptured by him and willingly gave my full attention to his words. He spoke of the ancient promise he was instructed to give to Enoch concerning this time of awakening I was experiencing now. He told me of the others that I would join, soon, who had also been summoned to this particular place, the training ground for our future tasks. Everything he shared gave me great comfort as I learned more about that which I'd always suspected.., my life, indeed, was unique.

...Angels Return to Lalibela, *again*.

We descended from atop Bête Golgotha. Weightless, with little thought to the impossibility of our flight as if in a slow moving elevator. Once on the ground, I noticed for the first time in the evening dusk, the three others that were already sitting lotus positioned on the solid rock floor outside the entrance to the church. With hardly a thought, they stood in tandem and knelt on their knees as if this move was totally natural and practiced. I found myself, immediately in sync with them and knelt, too.

Uriel turned to enter the ancient structure and with one downward motion of his hand, the door swung open with a gentle force. As we approached the entrance, we moved instinctively again as a group to remove our shoes and we filed into the narrow opening, singularly, as the others allowed me to follow first behind Uriel. I didn't ask for this honor, nor did I think about it, in the moment, but I now know that was a harbinger of things to come.

Beyond the narrow passage way, we entered into the heart of the church and immediately I was overcome by the sheer beauty of the room. Its ceiling was the roof where we had originally stood which means the entire structure was hollow from floor to ceiling. How was this place excavated? How were the windows on all four sides, from floor to ceiling, carved? I imagined the work that it must had taken to carve around and inside this structure leaving it totally attached in its base and concluded it could only have been done with divine assistance. There were flowers carved around each ascending window on all sides and I saw all the religious symbols of the world faiths on the walls. The crescent moon and star of Islam, the Star of David of Judaism and crosses adorn the floor, walls and ceiling.

The room illumined as we entered as if a dimmer had gradually been turned up, without a clear source of Light... until I saw that each one us were filled with Light. Suddenly, I felt as if I was in another one of my dreams, totally immersed in the impossibility of what I was experiencing. In my attempt to make sense of that experience, suddenly the room filled with music, more beautiful than any I'd ever heard. I looked around, then up to see the source of the music and was amazed that the vacant ceiling I had just viewed was now filled with a heavenly chorus of angelic hosts.

That alone would have been enough, but where there's music.., there is

GOD.

...GOD in the Temple

How do I describe the thing that's indescribable? Thankfully, I don't have to, because no sooner had we felt the presence of the Heavenly Father, we lost consciousness. Each of us fell to our face, overwhelmed by the sheer Power and Glory of His Majesty. We remained there in our humbled states, while He instructed Uriel and when we were finally summoned back to our reality, GOD and the angelic hosts had left the building. Uriel was given the task of messenger, again, but everything he was given to say, confirmed my worst fears concerning our uniqueness. Each of us had been brought to this sacred ground to be given a unique assignment. In fact, without another word being spoken, we discovered that the dormant gifts in each of us had been activated. GOD had come not just into the rock hewn temple, but into the temple of our very souls. No one could be in the presence of GOD and not be forever changed, forever altered, especially those with our unique DNA coding. I had come to Ethiopia to discover more about my visions only to learn that the answers I sought were always locked in me. In retrospect, I'm glad I wasn't given the vision of my exact future for fear I would have never desired to return home, to become the catalyst for what was to come.

No, in this particular case, ignorance was bliss. I sat there in the darkening temple, listening to Uriel give us the history of the creation of Lalibela, told as only one could from firsthand knowledge. I learned that throughout the earth there were other places that GOD had left as monuments to the Glory of Man as testaments to what could be accomplished when our inherent talents connected to the Ultimate Source. The Wonders of the World, as many had come to be known. Most of their creations had been attributed to others sources, such as aliens, in the feeble attempts of man to explain their existence.

But few, if any, have ever been attributed to GOD. Because of this continual disrespect, GOD has finally decided to activate the descendants of these lost kingdoms to build, again, one last tribute to Him. Those would be awakened that possessed within their genetic coding the blueprints of this final tribute and soon each would be call upon to fulfill their ancient destinies.

The more I desired to understand, the less I did.

As soon as our session with Uriel came to an end, abruptly each of us was transported back to our place of origin to awaken from our sleeps as though we had been only dreaming for the past two days.

...Atavist Awakened

I awoke, drenched in sweat, sensitive to the morning light –
and if I didn't recall that I was three years sober, I might have
assumed I was nursing a hangover.

But I did remember.

More than a dream, my body felt the effects only an abrupt
exertion, a surge of adrenaline can produce – something was
present I had not sensed before. I felt strangely 'alive' and it
was that heightened awareness that caused the morning light
to be more intense than in recent memory – if ever.

As I walked past the vanity, thinking only of the warm water
awaiting me in the my shower, I caught a glimpse of someone I
hadn't seen in more than a few years – I was looking at a man
I hadn't been for some time, now. *Overnight*, I seemed to have
aged, *in reverse!* The body staring back at me belonged to
me, yes, but the me of '19' – not that I'd let myself go totally at
26 – but my recent troubles had not allowed me to exercise as
I once did. Before that, the college drinking, poor diet and late
night studying of med school had begun to exact a physical
toil. The man reflected back to me now was only in my
memory, *'till now.*

Standing in that stream of hot liquid, I was washing away more than the night sweats. It felt as if the man I had been, all the mornings before now, was disappearing as quickly as the water circling the drain. Emerging naked into my bedroom, I had the sense of an open window on a wintry day – except it was the month of July. With no thought to my exposure, I stepped out onto the terrace, into my back yard – needing instinctively to bathe my body in the sun, to feel my feet in the warm grass. The rays of Light struck me like a bolt – and coursed through my whole being charging me from within. No, this wasn't mere arousal, it was electric – a current that stimulated my muscles, every muscle save my maleness, which remained totally unaffected. Whatever this was, the signal wasn't centered in my brain.., but the origin seemed to be the Sun itself – not just my imagination.

Stepping quickly back indoors, I felt an immediate lessening in intensity, but still a presence that led me to reach out to hold onto something as my body started to convulse – my back bending making me fall to by knees as I might in prayer. The heat beneath my skin shifted and centered in my back, where my shoulder blades burned without pain.
Then, I heard it again – the sound from the earlier dream. That same pulsating, rushing sound but this time, not in my dreams.., nor at a distance, but totally present.., near – 'till I realized that I was creating that displacement of wind and space – that pulsating was coming *from me,* by newly formed WINGS – extending from my searing back, just beneath my shoulders.

Everything in my room was disturbed, especially my bed which was swept back with the gentle force of a tempest wind – without thought I turned back in the direction of my terrace – an shot out in the morning air again, but this time my feet never touched a single blade of grass. As I soared out into the expanse, faster than humanly perceptible, I had a sense that I wasn't alone. When I ceased to move, but hovered just beyond the first barrier of clouds, I saw the others as they equally acknowledged my presence.

Startling, each hanging above his country of origin – beautiful and magnificent, poised as if for battle – now activated, awaiting, anticipating...

The whirling and power filled sounds that awoke me from my dreams that I now understood also safely ushered me home were tangible, present and ...Real.

"It's TIME."

...Another Awakens

"Time to wake up!!"

If this was to be like all the other mornings, I had at least two more of these before I truly had to respond. Besides, my bed always felt the most comfortable, this time of morning.

"I said, GET UP !!"

Wow, I guess I had slept through the first one. As I rose to go into the bath room and slowly awaken my slumbering body, I became painfully aware that not all of me was still asleep. No one had adequately warned me about turning 13. Not only did my dream life dramatically improve, this morning greeter was an unexpected bonus and once I figured out how to lessen its rigidity, I looked forward to its greeting each and every morning.

Standing before my toilet, helping it to subside before I could take my morning leak.., I slowly focused on the horizon just outside the window above my toilet. So cool, now, since my intense growth spurt that I could truly look directly out having grown six inches in one summer. Most guessed my age around 17 even with the appearance of my young face, just assuming I couldn't shave, but standing a tad over six feet, now, they always thought I must be older than 13.

Had I been older, I don't think I would have immediately screamed 'MOM!!' as loudly and certainly not as quickly, as I did. Almost too late did I remember my original purpose for straddling my toilet and quickly tucked away my less erect companion before my mother burst into my bathroom with a look of sheer panic in her eyes.

"What's wrong, Damon??!!" She was truly frightened as I had not called out to her like that since I was a little boy awaken by those horrible dreams that use to visit me nightly.

"Mom.., what's that.., in the sky??".., my trembling hand, pointing beyond the window, above my toilet.

Before she could scold me for my unusual outburst and release a tirade of warnings about my late night TV viewing habits or my tardiness for breakfast and school.., she came closer to see what I was transfixed at viewing. I can't be sure who screamed first, my mother or older sister who, overhearing me, had gone to the patio door next to kitchen to look out. But hearing them both scream, at the same time, I secretly wished that my Father was still alive to come into my room and awaken me from my nightmare, like he used to.

But this time, I knew this was no dream. In fact, I knew exactly what I was seeing perched in the morning sky. I knew, too, this day would come as certainly as I knew that every morning for the rest of my life, I would be greeted by my morning friend. Turning 13 had awakened much more in me than just my physical body.., my mind was processing this visual image with a particular intensity that gave me answers to questions I didn't even know to ask.

What's happening to me? What is this energy I feel?
Before I could process it at all, I felt the cold porcelain tile give way beneath my feet as the floor seemed to disappear and my young six foot frame crumpled into a heap on it.

Oh, no.., my sister is going to think I fainted!!, was the final thought rushing through my head as I slowly lost consciousness.

~:~

As I slowly came to, still on my bathroom floor, I knew the world had changed in a span of seconds as I realized my head was resting in my sister's lap and she was gently pressing a cool cloth on my forehead. The tenderness and fear in her eyes was disarming as my sister had taken a much harden approach to me after the death of our father and I was no longer treated tenderly by her, but was often scolded and ridiculed for being a baby at every turn. This was the grandest of all opportunities, but instead of capitalizing as only she could do, she was truly concerned for me.

"Ma.., Damon's awake!!"

Before I could make sense of it.., my mother appeared in the doorway, quickly assessed that I was okay and told us both, to come into her bedroom, *now*. Tossing over her shoulder as she disappeared that 'it' was all over the news.

For the next few hours, we all huddled in my mother's bed like we used to do as kids on those rare occasions she and our dad would allow us to join them. Those are some of my most favorite memories of dad...

As we lay there, listening to the news, we were mesmerized that everyone, all around the world, awoke in pretty much the same fashion today. All eyes and cameras were now pointed to the sky as the *Four Angels of the Apocalypse,* as they're being referred to by those leaders of various religious doctrines, hovered above in their designated positions. The whole world seems to have been placed on pause, as all attention was focused on the sky and the pundits that attempted to explain the phenomenon.

Instinctively, I knew that they weren't correct in any of their conclusions, but who was going to listen to a 13 year old boy even if he had grown six inches in one summer??

This time, just looking older, wasn't going to be nearly enough. How will I explain what I was shown in that brief time I laid on those cool tiles?

How do I tell them what EdenDust told me to reveal?

He warned me to not be afraid, but who is ever going to believe me, a 13 year old, trapped in a 17 year old body, with now, the mind of a professional scholar?

Indeed, who is going to listen to *me*?

...a Visitor in EDEN

"Damon, Wake Up."

I must have hit my head when I *fainted*. Okay, I can admit it. I'm not proud of it, but there it is. But before I can truly come down on myself for being a frighten boy again after all this time, I become aware that I'm not in my bathroom, anymore.

"You're okay, Damon. You're safe."

I know that voice, but I haven't heard it in a really long time. How many times did that voice soothe me back to sleep? But how can that be? I was seven when I was pulled from school and told my father had been killed on his last tour of duty. Clearly, this can't be real. Besides that, *this place* isn't supposed to be real, either. Not after all this time, this place can't be real. As I focus on my surroundings, I am gradually being placed at ease even though I'm obviously not in the comfort of my home anymore. I think to myself, "this place is familiar 'tho I haven't seen it in many years" and no sooner do I have that casual thought, there's a different voice, responding.

"Yes, you've been here, before. You used to play here quite frequently. The bridge between your world and this one was simple when you were younger. I apologize for using your father's voice to comfort you, but I thought it would also awaken your dormant memories."

"EDENDUST, is that you??"*

"Yes, Damon. Welcome home."

All at once, the memories rushed in. Every night of my young life, I visited this other world that I allowed myself to believe was all a dream as I grew older. The nightmares that ensued wasn't from being frightened I would, too, remember. I cried from having to leave this place and awaken in my darkened room. It was only the presence of my father that comforted me and reminded me that I was needed in that world more than in EDEN. When my father died, I felt I couldn't visit EDEN anymore, for fear I would never leave it, knowing instinctively, that I had to be totally present for my mother and sister. So I forced the dreams away from me and proceeded to forget that I had ever been to a place called EDEN.

"Damon, it's time for you to remember it all. Especially the games you used to play here in the Garden of EDEN. Those games will be the key to helping your world understand what's about to happen to them."

Remembering how time works in EDEN, I'm sure I probably wasn't passed out much longer than ten or fifteen minutes back on my bathroom floor.., but I felt as if I was spending hours with my old friend. He took me for a walk and while doing so, he awoke all of those dormant memories I had stored away all those years. I knew he was right to abruptly awaken me, but now that I was awakened, I also knew that when I returned, I would awaken to a world of fear and misinformation. I was assured that once I found my first audience, the rest of the world that needed to hear my message, would find me.

"Do the hard thing first.., and the rest will appear easy."

EdenDust always had a way with words. I suppose he should being one of two given the power of language *in the beginning*. I had come to trust him in my young memory and I fell right into step with him, now, without hesitation. I knew the coming upheaval was necessary and I knew that if I did not speak up immediately upon my return, there would be a price to pay that I wouldn't find too pleasing. I had disobeyed once before.., when I was told to tell my father to remain home with us and take a job on base that would have kept him safe. My disobedience carried a price that I felt was terribly unfair and I said so, vowing then to never return to EDEN and to forget it ever existed. I kept my part of the bargain so well that no sooner than I had defied my heavenly friends, my present world started to unravel.

When I awoke this morning to see one of those friends, Dathan, hovering in the air just outside my window, I exclaimed as I did not in fear as much as in shock at the flood of memories that came rushing in, ...so many at once that they caused me to pass out. Awakening, here, in EDEN, after all those years, I can only know that to be allowed back, now, was important. Recognizing Dathan as I fleetingly did also reminded me just how innocent we all were when we first met in EDEN and were given glimpses of this future day in the games we played. To have those two separate worlds, become one was overwhelming.

I just can't believe it's all about to go down, just as we've been told it would. So as my old friend, shared with me that I must speak up.., I knew I would, this time, without hesitation.

...suffer the Children

"Mom.., I know *who* they are."

The words were difficult to say, especially considering that in saying them, I was about to shatter my safe little home with a truth that just might not be able to be received.

I shifted my position on the bed to face my mom and sis and they instantly gravitated to one another, recognizing that I was speaking with more authority than I had ever before. The moment was also intensified as it was the first words I'd spoken since my exclamation and eventual collapse. I had their attention and suddenly I knew what my friend had said was true.

"Do the hard thing, first.., and the rest will appear easy."

I told them about my dreams as a boy. Why I cried each time I awoke. I talked with determination, fearing that if I stopped, I wouldn't finish.., or tell it all. When I got to the part about Dad, I saw my mother's eyes well up with tears. My sister showed the flash of the anger I had come to know, but both remained quiet.., allowing me to get it all out, without interruption.

When I finally fell silent, it was my mother who spoke. She measured her words carefully and my sister and I were about to learn exactly why she had seemingly been harder on me, all these years.

"Damon, as incredible as all of this might appear, in light of the activities of this day, your tale doesn't come close to what I, too, must reveal. I am not your mother.., well, not technically. I have always felt betrayed by your birth. As hard as that may to hear from your mother, it's time you know fully what has been the source of our tension.., the distance between us. While I always knew there would come a day when I could no longer keep from you the unnatural occurrences that surrounded your inception and birth, I secretly wished, no *Prayed*, that day would never, ever come."

She reached over and grabbed my sister's hand, knowing that what she was about to share was going to shatter everything that she had come to believe was normal in her life.., as if the morning we'd shared hadn't already done that!

"I was pregnant, with what we were told was another girl, two years after your sister's birth. Being only two years old, I'm sure Rachael has no memory of this, but I was in my seventh month and we had already started to put together the nursery, feeling lucky that we didn't have to shop for all new items. This particular evening, I had just washed all of Rachael's baby clothes that we would recycle and I was folding them and putting them into the little chest we had found over the weekend in a yard sale. Your father was in the garage, putting the crib together when I suddenly heard a voice calling to me. I felt a chill as the voice addressed me as no one had since my father had passed.

"Samantha James".

No one called me by that name, but dad. To all others, I had been Sammy Jo, since I was a toddler. My dad was so disappointed to learn that I was a girl and not the boy he'd hoped for, he refused to give up the name, Samuel James, he had chosen for the birth of his only son. In complete defiance, he always used that name and it was a constant reminder that I would never fully live up to his expectations for being born female.

So hearing that name, understandably, my hair stood on end.

As I turned to face the origin of the voice, I was immediately placed at ease in the midst of seeing a stranger in my nursery, as I beheld the most beautiful man I had ever seen then, or since, simply standing before me. He apologize for using the voice of my father, only meaning to place me at ease, while still getting my attention. He explained that he was a messenger of God, giving me his name as *Uriel* and he proceeded to tell me that I needed to stop preparing for the birth of a daughter. My child would be born male, instead, he proclaimed. Now, remember, I was in my seventh month and I knew without a doubt I was carrying a daughter. I thought to dispute his declaration, but instinctively, I held my peace. I listened to him continue with a certain set of instructions that I was to follow in the raising of this 'son', but I can tell you that in my heart, I knew then and there he had to be mistaken, so I only pretended to listen, perhaps in part because of the pain I'd endured by my father's obvious disappointment in not having a son. I knew I would do everything in my power to prove him wrong, which also meant I would not be party to your dad's disappointment if I told him, now, what I'd been told and this vision had less than favorable results. So I hid all of this from him, and myself, for the remainder of my pregnancy.

We continued to prepare for the birth of our daughter.

The night I went into labor and we went to hospital, I still believed that all that I thought I had experienced was nothing more than a mild hallucination as I'd not had another visitation since that first and fateful one. Only when the doctor announced with utter shock that I had given birth to a son, did I realize how my disobedience to divulge the visitation would be viewed, if I told your father, so it was a secret that I thought I might be able to keep all the way to my grave.

When your dad passed, I was racked with guilt that he never knew all the circumstances surrounding your birth. I also felt guilt every time you had those recurring dreams, which is why I never came to you in the night, but would send him, instead. I knew that I couldn't hear your tales of this other place, first hand, that he often shared with me, knowing fully that it truly existed and one day, you'll have to return to it, as I was told before your birth. I would like to think I was protecting you, but I know now, I was selfish and foolish to think that I could stand against what Uriel had told me. I felt I had a right to spend as much time as I could with you once your father died; especially knowing fully what was to come.

Why do you think I wasn't there with you when you awoke, moments ago? I was told, that when you turned 13, your real purpose would be revealed. Seeing those angels hovering in the air, I knew that your time with us was also coming to an end."

It was my turn to be silent as tears welled up in my eyes.

All those years I suppressed the truth of my dreams from myself and told myself that I had to be 'normal' for my family, was time lost. So much I had hidden. Things like my ever increasing intellect that seemingly grew in ways that was unnatural, I had learned to hide with little intentional mistakes, so I would fit in with the rest of class at school. Things like my gifted athletic prowess that I, too, pretended came harder than it ever did. I understood so much, now, that I never wanted to face before. But before I could place blame, I only thought of my sister, who was staring at both of us, as if she was seeing us for the first time. My heart broke for her, knowing that she didn't have my dreams, or Mom's vision as an anchor, now, and so her pain must be unbearable to have her safe world totally shattered without and now also, within.

I reached out to her, but she pulled away from us both and stood up from the bed, breaking the spell of our sudden bond and unity of truth.

Again, EdenDust's words came to me;

"Do the hard thing, first.., and the rest will appear easy."

Indeed, it would be my sister, not my mother that would be the first hurdle I would have to overcome, if I was ever able to be successful in sharing all I knew to the rest of the world. This challenge was made easier knowing for the first time there was nothing between me and my mother, anymore, now that the chasm that seemingly defined our existence had been bridged with our true confessions. With her help, we would reach our sister, but first, I had to tell her about the vision I had just had about my present and future role in it the coming events.

This would prove to be the easiest part of my morning.

...a Family United

I still sat perched at the end of my mother's bed. She was lying back on her pillow with the covers jumbled between her legs. She was dividing her time between the muted TV and my story that, like before, I was telling as quickly as I could breathe the words. I had so much to say, stories that only me and father had shared. I found out, while I spoke, that some of the things I'd shared where familiar, my father had shared with her, 'tho purposely left out much, to lessen the idea that I was truly a troubled little boy. I can only imagine how tempting it must had been for my mother to not divulge her secret, but knowing how protective my father was toward me, he might have felt betrayed and taken me away from this home that I so desperately needed today, more than ever.

When I found a proper place that allowed me to pause, my mother, hearing it all, said the most peculiar thing in response.

"We need to visit your father's grave, one last time, as a family."

In that simple statement, was her blessing for me to continue on my path..., no fanfare, no pleading for more time, or questions about the details I obviously couldn't share.

Nothing, but a graceful resignation that our family was about to dissolve into nothingness, along with the rest of the world, and that we might 'live' on, but this unit would never be the same. She knew that she would pay a price for her disobedience, but until that fateful moment, she was resigned to be a family, one final time.

As she made her way to the kitchen, I turned around to view the TV for the first time since I had turned by back to it to announce my intimate knowledge of the day's activities. It would appear that the whole world had come to a halt. The stocks had plummeted, as fear cause many to withdraw their life's savings, as if having the money in hand would matter, unaware that their very actions had devalued all that they thought they were protecting. All the services of the governments had come to halt, so all those dependant on their monthly stipends were desperately trying to find assistance from any other sources they could. Churches had to turn away anyone who wasn't already a member of their congregation, having only limited resources for all those that had given their life savings to sustain their church homes for a time such as this. Anger, fear, mistrust, desperation was on face after face, as everyone blamed another for this final state of the world.

In the end, the overwhelming consensus was that everyone was in the exact same position. The priest and prostitute, the pimp and CEO, the teacher and the illiterate, the professor and student.., all were looking literally to the heavens for understanding.., and instruction.

A Family United, finally.

I thought to myself, as I turned to leave and find my sister and mother that it was always going to end like this.

Didn't anyone think the Book of Revelation was real?

~:~

Standing over my father's grave, I read the inscription now, with even more understanding.

I gave my all for my country and my family.
I loved and lost all, in the end.

I remember how my mother fought with the lawyers about putting that fully on his tombstone. I was only seven at the time, but I knew that it held a meaning that truly hurt my mother, particularly. Today, we would learn what that battle was truly about. My sister had spoken only a few words since our revelations and now seemed to be just going through the motions. At 15, I'm sure she was feeling like she just wanted to return to bed and awaken from this protracted dream. But feeling the presence of Dathan who's hovering seem to follow everyone like the eyes of the Mona Lisa, didn't allow many errant thoughts and flights of fancy, having his constant reminder of our eminent demise.

"I never wanted him to serve his country," my mother mumbled.

Perhaps I should have known this, but I didn't. I could tell by my sister's reaction this was news to her, as well. My mother had always seemed particular relieved when dad left for his tour of duties but this, again, was her particular strength..., misdirection.

"I was different after your birth, Damon.

Understanding the burden I carried, now, you two might understand. He was truly unhappy with me more and more for not shaking off what he thought was the post partum blues. My secret was destroying us, but loving his family as he did, he felt the only way to truly provide for us was by enlisting. It seemed to be the best of both worlds.., peace for me, and money for his family. But he hated not being near both of you. In fact, he had decided to leave active duty. He had also decided that if I no longer wanted him as a husband, he would rather be near his children, than serving another tour of duty. The papers were all signed for both to become reality, but I convinced him that we needed more time, to break the news of the divorce to both of you, being only seven and nine at the time. So, he withdrew all the paperwork and returned to active service, obviously delaying the divorce as well.

I felt like the biggest hypocrite, enduring all the pomp and circumstance of burying a fallen soldier. The pension felt like blood money that I hadn't earned. When I read what his final wish was in the two short verses he wanted on his tombstone, I knew that he was reaching out from the grave for the truth to be told about not only who he was, but what he had endured and sacrificed. To think I tried to even deny him that ...well, today, I need to say to both of you that I'm sorry for not being a more loving mother and the wife your father deserved. I suppose it's all too late, now. But you need to know, finally, your father loved you both.., and even loved me, in the end, for he never forced me to divulge my true face, publicly or privately.

The blood curdling scream that my sister let out, pierce the dusky sunset and knowing instinctively that this wasn't just teenage angst but an ancient and dormant evil lurking beneath her seemingly calm exterior, caused me to take a defensive step backwards, in preparation for the battle that would ensue. But, as prepared as I was for this ultimate family encounter, I wasn't prepared for my mother's swift action. In one movement, she turned toward my sister while simultaneously pushing me aside. She stood toe to toe with her and in a voice I'd never heard before; she called the demon by name.

"Come out *Azazyel* !! Leave her, now!
Let Rachael Be!!"

At the exact moment of this declaration, Dathan shifted his gaze in the heavens to our location and in one swift motion, he passed over the graveyard, just in time to grab hold of the spirit as it departed my sister and in one movement he flung it into the heavens with the force of a missile. As my sister lay limp on the grass, my mother then turned to me and immediately I knew I was in the presence of another, not my mother.

"We've never met, Damon, but I am Gabriel. Forgive me for needing to appear so quickly that I didn't have the luxury of time to make a personal appearance. We've been monitoring everything about you and you were in imminent danger from those that do not wish for you to fulfill your destiny and were attempting to possess your sister in hopes of delaying your journey. It's time for you to come to us. Say goodbye to your mother, as I briefly return her to you."

I knew in a moment, my mother was back with the most amazed look of sorrow and bewilderment in her eyes, having been an unwilling witness and participant in the recent events. I hugged her and kissed her tear-laced face. I then knelt down and kissed my dazed sister's forehead. I told them to be strong in the coming days and reminded them that they were now the last of our family and to love and forgive one another.

I reached out to touch my father's tombstone and just as I barely felt the coolness of the marble on my fingertips, I was gone, caught up in the vortex that I would come to know as Gabriel, the most powerful angel in all the Heavens.

I barely had time to steal a final glimspe of my earthly family before I was speeding toward my command audience with Gabriel.

In dramatic fashion, I was about to be fully introduced to the rest of my heavenly family.

BOOK THREE
Prologue:

I'm sure most of you might recall from your Sunday school classes reading stories about *legions of Angels*. The portraits usually showed about ten angels in the heavens all looking sweet and angelic-like. While there are moments when they will appear that way, I would be remiss if I didn't write that when you actually see a legion of angels, it's a most terrifying sight. The power represented is unprecedented. Just one Arch Angel alone could completely destroy one of your urban cities. You can only imagine the destruction generated by a Legion. But here they were, hovering before me in EDEN.

Waiting...

When Uriel was given permission to awaken Dathan, they began gathering just above the expanse of EDEN in anticipation of finally being unleashed to fulfill their divine purpose. Knowing that My Father was preparing to destroy the Earth was one thing, but seeing the instruments to that very destruction poised before me was undeniable.

Earth would soon know fully the Power of GOD.

The plan was truly set into motion when I was allowed to awaken young Damon. Seeing him return to EDEN was joyous, even for that brief moment. How I had grown to love him as his spirit would often come and visit with me and the others as he easily traversed the chasm being our worlds on his nocturnal visits from his earthly home. It was beautiful for us to behold all the atavists come and go and play so freely and joyfully in what they only remembered as 'dreams' once they awakened. But everyone who encountered him could always sense the power that lay dormant in Damon, but we always felt that he truly believed he was 'just a boy' having fanciful dreams. We knew that one day he would be awakened to truly take his rightful place. The only other that could possibly understand what he was about to go through is the only other one ever allowed to be flesh *and spirit*.

Was the world ready to also know that God had two sons, Jesus, the Christ..., and **Damon** ?

...in GOD We Trust

Gabriel is about to speak and with one wave of his hand, he commanded the full attention of every warrior angel.

"He was born a boy, generated from a womb that was already in possession of a female child.
He contains, in him, the very essence of maleness and femaleness,
He possesses the ability to create life and equally destroy it, with a thought.
In Him, GOD has placed the knowledge of Good and Evil.
In Him is the Tree of Life.
As our Father prepares the utter destruction of Mankind and their original dwelling place,
And EDEN, the new earth, is being readied for all the inhabitants that will be saved,
GOD has transferred the sacred part of all that was hidden and protected in the Garden of EDEN, into this living being, born of flesh and spirit,

...and his name is ***DAMON***."

Hearing Gabriel speak of me in that moment, everything I was, that I remembered of my earthly existence, evaporated and my full attention turned to the Source of Illumination that filled the Heavens, for just over my shoulder, on His Throne, was GOD, with Jesus, sitting on his right side.

The Heavens came alive with singing and instrumentation of all kinds.., the powerful Legion, bowed down.., and as I began to kneel, GOD called me by name and waved me closer to the throne.

There, in the Glory of Jesus and my Heavenly Father, and in the presence of my old friend and teacher, *EdenDust*, and all the mighty warrior angels, I, Damon, neared The Throne of GOD and stood in silent awe.

I wasn't afraid, strangely, as the sheer majesty of it all calmed my heart.

"Damon, *my son*, in you, too, I am well pleased.

You have carried the treasures given to you, with honor.

I awaken the fullness of them, now.

It's TIME for you to take your rightful place.

I, Damon, in adoration of My Father and in respect to My Brother, walked forward in total understanding and acceptance, and humbly sat in my rightful place *on the left side of the Throne.*

...as it is in HEAVEN

I would love to say that I'd been waiting for this day. But that just hadn't been my experience. Unlike Jesus, I never knew my connection to GOD. I was allowed to have the fully man experience that Christ never got to know. His purpose for coming to the earth was to 'redeem' it back to GOD by dying for the sins of mankind, instead, fulfilling the penalty for the sin debt my Father had established. My existence on earth was totally that of a young boy, growing up and experiencing life on his own terms, in the confines of his earthly family's structure. With the exception of my unusual dreams, I can't say that I ever had any idea that this would be my lineage. While living as I was, I had unknowingly become the advocate to the world that it would need in this, their darkest hour. I was groomed to be the bridge between Heaven and earth. Before you think this totally puts my brother out of a job.., you should only be reminded that when He appears again, it's to bring total judgment on earth. So, in essence, you might call me the opening act!

While in Heaven with my Father and Brother, I learned of their plans for saving as many on earth as possible. I'm instructed to return to now, and build what might come to known as a virtual 'ark', to collect the souls of those that truly wish to denounce the wickedness and godlessness of the world system and finally acknowledge GOD as their Lord and Savior. Less you think that I appear as a young boy still, even in my tall statue, know that the presence of Dathan and his fellow companions 'poised and waiting' have been a daily reality for *nearly a year, now*, in what has appeared as a brief moment in time in Heaven.
But something changed in me, when GOD awakened the fullness in me...

I come back to earth, fully man, now.

Much of the world came to the knowledge of GOD out of fear, but surprisingly just as many returned to business as usual viewing the angels' presence with no more than a cursory glance. To say this angered my Father doesn't come close to describing the tremendous restraint He's exhibited to remain on His original timetable and plan for earth's destruction.

EdenDust has told me, before my birth on earth, there were similar moments of utter desolation and destruction where man has shown an uncanny ability to adapt toward their lesser state of existence over time. Perhaps it's been a flaw in the de-evolution of Adam's genetics, but soon all this will be history.

As I arrived at the center of the on-going debate and conferences on exactly *who the angels* were and just when their divine purpose and intention would be exposed, I knew exactly why I had been allowed to grow up as I had. I had been exposed to the insanity that often passed as logic, even genius, first hand as I watched my father and mother deal with the military, and one another. In this world, power always wins the argument, not rational logic and certainly never moral or ethical arguments. So entering this discussion, I knew that I had to establish my authority and credentials early on, or I would not be allowed a second listen.

"Do the hard thing first, and the rest will appear easy."

Thanks EdenDust.

America had taken a dominant position in the examination of the angels and what their presence meant, so naturally the world was focused on the findings of those conferences, centered in Washington DC. In the year that had followed their appearance, one man in particular had come upon the scene as prophesied, which many in church circles quickly identified as the *anti-Christ*, but to the rest of the world, he was simply the savior they had been waiting for. He was exactly the archetype you would come to expect that fallen man would choose for their 'leader'. Young, charismatic, rich, handsome and need I say, white and powerful, this Euro Prophet had appeared on the world stage in dramatic fashion.

~:~

Prince Philipp was already famous just being born of royalty. His father, King Harry, ascended the throne only *seven* years into the reign of his brother, William, who had become the most popular King in all of England's history. Only their father, King Charles, had a shorter time on the throne, dying one year and three months in office. Due to William's assassination, Harry was sworn in as King with considerably less fanfare that his older brother. The pomp and circumstance of William's coronation was rumored to be the most lavish in history. England was feeling particularly satisfied that the most beloved son was finally on the throne and the expectations ran high in anticipation of the type of King he would become at the young age of 42. But Prince Philipp, a young man of leisure at 15 at the time of William's coronation, despised his uncle, recognizing that his chances of becoming King were certainly growing more and more remote. He desired the power more than anything else, having been born in wealth and so, when he was approached by a secret group of powerful players in his late teens with an opportunity to usurp the throne, there wasn't a bit of hesitation in his answer.

The fact that the plan that was set into motion three years ago would have these present desired results.., well, no one could have foreseen this latest turn of events. I was about to experience especially that EdenDust, in showing me the history of the world, had prepared me greatly for this moment.

Prince Philipp's cohorts had arranged the assassination of King William, who had no heir, so that his least-liked father could take possession of the throne, unbeknownst to Harry. With him as King, all eyes immediately turned to Prince Philipp, who many felt would carry on the legacy of his beloved uncle who had fallen too soon. King Harry was amicable about it all, having lived in the shadow of his brother all his life, so why not his son, too? Besides, Philipp at 22, was still maturing and there was hope that with a little more time spent grooming his impetus son, the doubts of his child's leadership skills would dissipate with time. No one could have prepared him for the turn of events that were soon to follow.

EdenDust showed me that Prince Philipp was being pursued by an over enthusiastic fan on his motorcycle as he was being chauffeured in a motorcade enroute back to the palace after a night of fun and frolic. This evening wasn't unlike any of the previous ones, so when they entered the tunnel, the very place of his grandmother's fateful accident, no one would had gamble that this sacred location would once again be on all the news outlets at the crack of dawn. The motorcade swerving to miss the stalled car in the tunnel, meant the cyclist didn't have quite enough time to do the same and as his cycle flipped forward, it clipped the back of the car carrying Prince Philipp, which caused his driver to break too suddenly, locking the front breaks and sending their car flipping forward as well.

The call that awoke King Harry, immediately brought back the rush of emotions long suppressed, but hardly forgotten, of his mother's accident and he immediately felt a chill, recognizing the irony of the moment deeper than any.

His immediate concern went to his son, but at the same time, he felt a cruel hand of fate manipulating the public's sympathy much in the same way it had turned against his father in the wake of Princess Diana's accident. The desire for his brother, William, to become King started that very night in that tunnel and he couldn't help but feel that if Philipp survived, history was about to repeat itself.

Not only were King Harry's feelings dead on, they were eerily prophetic. EdenDust continued to reveal to me that Prince Philipp remained in a coma for three days with the minimalist of life signs. Many rumored that he had actually died, fueling the future hysterics that would ensue when he actually awoke and sat up and asked about the health of the motorcyclist.

That *resurrection* moment was broadcast 'live' as the media had been keeping constant vigil, as many feared this was not an accident but a near successful and perverted assassination attempt on Philipp's life, especially due to the location of the crash. The world demanded firsthand knowledge of Philipp's recovery, so to appease the world at large, King Harry allowed the constant monitoring of his son's vital signs as he recognized the folly in angering his son's loyal fans at this critical juncture. So, Philipp literally 'rose' from the dead in full view of the rest of the world and was immediately hailed as someone who might have answers beyond the grave concerning all that the world was experiencing.

This wasn't exactly the plan of those that had originally set all of this into motion with King Williams' death, but they were opportunists and certainly knew how to capitalize on the Prince's sudden infamy. The fact that the plan was accelerated in such a dramatic fashion should have been their first clue that this was no longer 'their game' but that of another that also was watching the hovering angels with a particular interest.

~:~

Allowing those fools to think they were geniuses was too simple.

Man had always responded greedily to a little whisper of power, so when Lucifer had appeared to them with a suggestion of eternal life and youth if this hidden committee could position Prince Philipp in line for the throne, it wasn't even put to a vote. All was going according to plan and few had ever thought twice about ordering the assignation of William. Their combined families controlled over 80% of the world's wealth and few ever experienced the emotion of 'regret', except when it pertained to a deal with an undesirable outcome. But the panic set in when the news made the rounds of Prince Philipp's near fatal accident. As the world watched his daily progress, so did they with particular interest, knowing instinctively that if he didn't survive, the 'deal' they'd made would become void as well. Upon seeing his *resurrection,* those that had paid attention to their early catholic school boy classes, knew then and there that they had made a deal with the devil.., and the worst was yet to come.

~:~

When Philipp asked of the cyclist's health, that one gesture was all the world needed to appoint him the coming 'messiah' that would save the world. The months that followed were a whirlwind of press and interviews that would rival a breakthrough in the cure for cancer or an undiscovered, inhabited planet in the present solar system. Philipp had easily become the most recognized man in the world and the symbol of 'hope' beyond this present day omen. The fact that he had access to untold wealth, made him of particular interest to those in power in Washington, which is why everyone was here, today, to hear him speak.

So much focus was on the 'son' that no one noticed when King Harry's plane landed secretly at a nearby base in Virginia and was slowly progressing in his motorcade toward the capital, while watching this conference with particular interest on close circuit in his private car.

In the middle of the night, I'd made my first stop back on earth in his chambers where I revealed the full plan of the dark forces that were set into motion with first the *murder* of his brother. King Harry's prayers had indeed reached Heaven and one of the first souls of the 144,000 that I was to gather *was his*. He heard in dismayed what he already feared and was fully prepared to do whatever he could to save the world, especially, it would seem, from his own son.

Now my presence in the audience was by design to eclipse this moment from becoming the triumphal victory Lucifer had planned by putting someone under his control into a position of sheer and unlimited power. With the father as an advocate of Heaven, this promised to turn into a royal battle of historic proportions before it was all said and done.

As I settled into my seat in this massive auditorium, I felt gratitude that EdenDust had done an excellent job preparing me for this moment since as a small child. I looked around the podium and immediately recognized the cast of characters that sat before me.

Government leaders and heads of state from the most powerful countries, dignitaries, professors, physicians and ministers, sitting next to poet laureates and Nobel prize recipients.., yes, I saw them all poised in anticipation for the keynote speaker...

The respected of the respected and every one of them,

...*wicked to their very cores.*

...Thy Kingdom Come

Prince Philipp was every bit as charming in person as you might expect.., but so was the serpent in the Garden and the analogy was an accurate one. For those without faith, or who had come to their faith fearfully, his demeanor of quiet confidence in the midst of the chaos would be a welcomed refuge. The fact that he was given the keynote speech was all the more evidence that the world was at a lost for tangible answers. The committee that had positioned the prince was also a pretty influential group and it was in their best interest to do the bidding of their master in order to assure their futures. Besides that, they had promised the conference that the prince would be making an announcement that would be of particular interest to the *World Bank*.

After the initial crash of the markets at the appearance of the angels, the banks of the world were *combined into one system* under the guise that it would allow a swifter recovery. Having the wealth centrally located allowed the not so secret ruling committee to truly make unilateral decisions now despite the leadership of any particular country. This new announcement undoubtedly would benefit those in power at the expense of the governing masses and yet here they were, in total compliance, chanting ...

"Philipp, Philipp"... like lambs to the slaughter.

Being able to appear fully human, allowed me to sit in the audience under the radar of those spiritual minions positioned as the prince's security team. I recognized them all as fallen angels who had more than earned their reputations as manipulators of minds and wills. If ever there was a doubt as to who was ultimately promoting the prince's agenda, the veil was about to be lifted permanently. As Prince Philipp was being introduced, I felt the presence of *that other* in this room. Not surprised at all that he would want to be present for his ultimate betrayal of man.

I was looking carefully at the Prince as he rose to take the podium after a video introduction that took us through his young life in the palace, his boarding schools, his military training and life of philanthropy before his fateful crash and subsequent coma. The audience had the expected reaction when the visual images showed his resurrection and burst into spontaneous (scripted) applause as he rose simultaneously and started his walk to the edge of the stage.

I was looking for any sign in him that he was doing any of this under duress. The man that stood before us was as calm as anyone could possibly be, being trussed into the spotlight as dramatically as he was. If he had any clue that he was being used by others, he didn't seem to betray it in his calm demeanor and solemn gaze. If I had never seen what true peace and humility looked like, I, too, might have been persuaded that this man could really be the Messiah, too.

Standing at the edge of the stage, waiting ever so patiently, listening, 'till the room fell perfectly still, Prince Philipp finally began speaking in an incredible hushed tone, as if he was getting use to his own voice.

"Who am I, to tell you, that we're in trouble?

But the trouble I speak of isn't from our heavenly visitors that have captured our attention since their fateful presence in our skies. It seems to me that we're in trouble *from OURSELVES*. Those angelic creatures have done nothing to us, but if their very presence is enough to send our markets crashing in a day.., We are indeed in trouble.
If, without ever setting foot on our beloved soil, we have allowed them to strike fear in hearts..,
We are in trouble.
If we have seen our coming together as a last ditch effort to save ourselves, the lesser of evils..,
We are in trouble.

BUT, if instead you see yourselves, as I see you, as I see 'US', you would know that our *unity* now, is our very strength against all the forces that have convened to destroy us.

I see that their presence did *NOT* destroy us, but in essence did the impossible, the unthinkable.., showed us that it was our age old differences had been the source of all of our troubles.
Recall now, the expense of all the separate governments, militaries, health agencies and how the misdirection of all of those resources had weakened us?
Those beings did not crash our markets!!
We did!!
Those beings did nothing but reveal our own fears and doubts and frustrations. If we learn nothing from this past year, take it from one who knows firsthand that our time on this earth is not a guarantee, but while we are here;

WE are in control of our own destiny.
WE, moving as one body, with one mind and purpose, can build ANY thing WE desire.
WE can heal our world of all its ills if WE remember the lessons learned in this year.

Let's use all these conferences to ask another question, a different question, one that doesn't center on what 'going' to happen to us.., but what are we GOING to do with this time, now that we've been formally introduced to one another? What are we willing to do *to save ourselves*?
Are we ready to use our common fear of the unknown and turn that into our strength and not our weakness?
If you are.., then I have a plan for our futures, but I am not going to waste one minute of our time together discussing that which we cannot fully know. I wish for you to examine yourselves, now, in this moment of silence and I ask you to do one thing for me.., search within your own hearts to see if you believe that we must accept responsibility for ourselves.., and in a moment, I will tell you what I truly believe we can do, to move ourselves *from fear to Victory.*"

Observing this brilliant manipulation, I understand one of the reasons I've been allowed to remain fully man is to experience how the human mind works. Everyone fully connected to GOD deals with absolutes. There are no shadows in serving GOD or believing in Him. It is just a matter of will and once given, it is given fully in mind, body and soul.
Man, however, can say something in mind, and never fully embrace it in soul. Everyday man has to renew their minds to serve or believe. This fatal flaw has been capitalized upon to varying degrees by those that have sought to manipulate or even destroy mankind and it's this same moment of indecision that's being so artfully manipulated today. Having never fully trusted or believed in GOD, even with the presence of the angels hovering nearby, allows Lucifer his greatest advantage, ever, to destroy Mankind by presenting them the ultimate gift, one of their own choosing.., *a False Prophet*. Without even hearing whatever the Prince has plans for beyond this pause in his message, the end result for all of those that choose to trust in him as their savior will be 'a kingdom on earth' that totally removes GOD from His Rightful place as Lord of their lives.

For this reason alone, I am here now: To ensure that there are *two* choices of servant hood, not just the one that's about to be proposed. As Prince Philipp continues, only I know that in actuality, this is all part of GOD's plan.

Yes, even this deception.

...Choose Ye, This Day

Philipp gazed out into the awaiting masses.

"Thank you for indulging me. Would you like for me to continue?'

What started out as a murmur, slowly built in intensity as the audience erupted in applause and affirmations of 'YES, YES.., YES!!!'

I didn't care much about those that were exclaiming at that time for my attention immediately had shifted focus on *those that did not stand.* In the swiftest of moments, I gathered each of their souls and sealed them for GOD before the ever watchful opposition had time to equally focus on them and mark them for later conquest. GOD's virtual ark had just gathered a few hundred more just in this room alone, but my spirit had sealed thousands that were watching via satellite that I equally sensed were not fully persuaded to trust in this 'man'.

Now the real battle lay before me, as the prince continued with the added strength of those who had just given him their wills. Some of them still had time to denounce allegiance, but it would be harder after this initial offering. Whatever was about to be proposed would prove more difficult to counteract without exposing myself fully. Paying particular attention to these next words was also another who had arrived quietly in the rear of the auditorium without fanfare. The prince father, King Harry, was present, finally, and with his appearance, all the players were finally in place.

Prince Philipp, embolden by the rapt attention and show of support, continued.

"Allow me to tell you, what I believe you just discovered hidden in your own hearts.

DOUBT.

What do you really believe to be possible, anymore?
You've trusted in your governments.., and they've failed you.
You've trusted in your synagogues and your churches, and sadly, they too have failed you in your darkest hours of need.
You thought the scholars would surely know what was happening, having devoted their lives to the study of all things unknown. But you find their answers suspect and lacking.
You even thought those that you loved would be able to protect you, but you find their presence equally disconcerting as they lean too heavily on you for answers.
Who can you trust? And can that gift of Faith be placed in something.., or someone, Tangible.., Present.., and equally invested in your outcome?

You DOUBT if there *is* such a person.., but you secretly pray that there is. Well, I have an answer for you..., and no, save those chants of Philipp, Philipp, Philipp... for the one who is going to truly save you...

Is, *YOU*.

Yes.., YOU.

Each one of you has dormant in him or her, the answer to today's problems.
I've already told you that if we combine our resources, our intellect, our faith.., we can move mountains.., and if not, mountains.., we can certainly force those angelic beings, those holy errand boys.., to go back from whence they came!!

I have a plan to unlock that hidden potential in each of you and once totally awakened, you will see your unlimited potential. In all your communities, right now, *Centers* have been established for you to enter, as soon as tomorrow morning, for each of you to be given the information you need to make this fateful next step. I know you're wondering what's going to happen.., how much is it going to cost.., what about my present job.., well, here's my gift to you. With the help of some pretty prominent benefactors that wish to remain anonymous, this is all being underwritten so that not only will it be 'free' to you.., we will actually pay for your training!

For those that are ill, or those that are thinking they don't have the ability to contribute.., believe me, your *Minds* are more important than your bodies and we'll explain more fully in our Centers how you'll be able to connect to the *Collective* from the comfort of your own home. Gone are the days of needing to wait for the government's monthly stipends. Once connected into this new consciousness, all your needs will be provided from food to healthcare, in exchange for your loyalty to our common interest of raising up ourselves as a divine force to reckoned with.

Being equal in every way, there will be no need to envy, to steal, to worry about those nagging necessities anymore, and our common connection will increase our productivity 200 fold. I came today, not to lead you.., but to inspire you and equip you to become all that you can be and there's no time like the present for you to stand up and say that you're ready for a new world and that world is in your power to create..,

NOW!"

And with that last exclamation, the world was totally in the wake of this new idealism. I could sense all over the planet the cheers for this misguided shepherd and his demonic plan and how he had, in one speech, given them everything they'd been primed to believe was the ultimate offering. Little did they realize what it was going to cost them, in the end.

But as I looked around the audience, I could see on the faces of many.., that they had already counted the cost of allowing this much intrusion into their personal lives. Funny how no one fully values just how precious freedom of choice really is until they are no longer in a position to demand it.

As each would soon discover upon entering those Centers tomorrow.., it's not their minds this consortium would be ultimately purchasing..,

but their souls.

~:~

As soon as Prince Philipp was whisked backstage.., there were questions being directed at him from every dignitary with most of their inquiries centered on being left out of the decision making process that created this global plan. The magnitude and scope of this was overwhelming, let alone the logistics of it all. How would this data be collected and how would it be used?? Prince Philipp immediately knew that each had their own agendas posed as inquiries and it was this thinking, this archaic business as usual model that he knew would be his greatest hurdle. No sooner than he had that thought and was considering his answers carefully, the room fell silent and he was no longer the center of attention as all eyes fell from him to the visitor that had entered this enclave of power.

There were only two men that could demand that kind of immediate attention and he knew the President wasn't in Washington. As he turned to follow the gaze of the room, he immediately felt small, in the presence of ...

"Hello, Father. This is a pleasant surprise. I didn't know you were coming to hear me speak."

"I'm many things, Philipp, but a fool isn't one of them", King Harry answered in a tone that caused most in the room to divert their attention downwardly.

Everyone that is, but Philipp, who continued to look at his father with innocent eyes, seemingly prepared for this moment that had been in the making for some time now. The Prince sensed this statement carried the weight of a full reckoning of his deeds and if that was the case, he didn't wish for this to play out publicly, especially now.

"Father, whatever do you mean.., and before you answer that, please be mindful that I'm on a tight schedule and since I didn't know that you would be in attendance..."

King Harry moved swiftly toward his son, cutting him off in mid-sentence. Philipp instinctively took a step backwards and immediately the dignitaries realized the shift in power. This was no longer a King and Prince before them.., but a Father and son and out of respect, they silently dispersed, just out of sight, but certainly not out of range of overhearing what they knew would be in their best interests to know about their 'new savior'.

King Harry stood silently, holding his son in his gaze as the rage built up in him to a point that had this not been his son, he surely could have strangled him with his bare hands. Philipp's protectors, the minions, stood just beyond the pool of light that bathed the twosome, awaiting their orders to move in, knowing that if they did, it would be an act of treason to attack the leader of a country. However, they were not waiting for a signal from Philipp.., but from *the other*.., who had decidedly emerge from his dark perch to witness this exchange, as well. Whatever the outcome, he was certain to have victory, feeling the rage in the father and the indignation in the son, both feeding into his insidious plans.

"How could you?" A simple question posed to his son, King Harry asked with intensity, his eyes locked fully onto his son, leaving Harry to wonder just what he might truly know.

Evasively, Prince Philipp responded, "Father, you must be more precise if there's something you truly wish to discuss, but as I've already said, I'm on a tight schedule. Perhaps we can continue this...."

King Harry struck his son with such force that the slap brought Philipp immediately to his knees. The magnitude of the moment was so humbling that before Philipp could rise, his father pressed his hand firmly into his shoulder forbidding him.

"How could you kill my brother.., *your uncle?*"

So, this is it.

This was the moment originally shown to me by EdenDust, where I am to enter the scene and formally introduce myself. The dark one is certainly feeling a sense of victory considering how in one more moment, kingdoms all over the world would topple if this scene were allowed to continue and if he unleashed his minions to intervene destroying all those within range of this tragic scene.

"Do the hard thing, first, and the rest will appear easy."

Recalling EdenDust's admonition, I moved forward, into the light and for the first time allowed others to behold me, as I truly am.

"Harry, I thank you for coming so quickly.
Philipp, please rise."

Suddenly the backstage was illumined in a way that only a heavenly presence could accomplish. My appearance and my informal greeting of the royal duo established me to be beyond the reach of all of those in rapt attention, while still remaining a mystery to all of them, *save one*. Recognizing me, Lucifer retreated and in doing so, his minions took his lead and stepped fully back into the shadows as well. Everyone anxiously listened to learn more about my sudden presence but they were equally interested to see how the rest of this tragedy would unfold.

Without hesitation, I spoke with all the authority of Heaven:

"We all have roles to play in the days to come that have been written and no amount of anger or indignation can change that. Harry, I know of your need for understanding and justice, but you'll never have it, this side of Heaven. Your son made his choice, long ago, and he serves the will of another who has only used him in a greater story that must be played out as it is written.

I speak directly to that one who has chosen to hover in the shadows. THIS IS NOT YOUR TIME and YOUR PRESENCE HERE IS NO LONGER WELCOMED.

The rest of you should know now that your choices in this day have already set into motion this ultimate battle for dominion over your world. But for those questions that have yet to be answered, know that I come, in the name of Heaven and all that is good and righteous to give you the answers that you seek, and prepare you for the future that is certain, despite the misguided efforts of these that refer to themselves as 'The Center'.

I Am Damon, and I ask that you listen, and heed my warning. If you proceed as you must, the end of your journey will be certain destruction. You have been given a choice that will fail to accomplish your personal goals, and will only in return strengthen those of another. Consider this as you leave this place now for your respective homes and countries and weigh your options carefully. There's much more to be lost than gained if you join forces to do battle against Heaven.

Isn't the presence of the Angels enough to deter you as surely you must realize that GOD is fully aware of you, even now, and certainly every action you take from this moment forward that pits your will against His is futile?

If I sound as if I speak with authority, it's true, I do.

I was born flesh and blood, here on your earth, and lived a normal life, but on the fateful day that the angels appeared in our heavens, that was also the birth of my awakening. I learned on that day, that I, too, am God's son, Damon, and my presence among you now is to prepare you for what's to come. *I was created to be a bridge between earth and Heaven* in order to give you the truth of what's been set into motion. There is no reference of me in any of your religious books for the secret of my existence was hidden from all except those that were with GOD, in the beginning. The role I was born to play in these end times is simple, I am here to offer you another option than the sole one presented to you, today, by Philipp and those whom he so willingly serves.

With all of your collective talents, your attempts to stand against GOD will fail. My presence here today is to remind you that My Brother, whose name is known throughout your world, will soon make His Presence known, here on earth, again. But upon His appearance, your destruction will be immediate. Choose wisely in this day, in whom you will serve."

How ironic to those in attendance backstage that the questions they all had in forming this conference were being answered fully for the first time, with authority. Still there were those that never desired the truth whose hearts were obviously set to capitalize on the fear and their reasons for being a part of these conferences were not only now exposed, but threatened. No sooner than I had ceased to speak, the murmuring began. *No one* spoke directly to me, but in essence treated my words with as much consideration as they had given the presence of the Angels. Mankind, once again, was showing its desire to never fully trust GOD or to trust in GOD despite their claims to do so on their currency.

Yet, I had given the added information to all the countries and dignitaries to take back to their constituents, if they so chose to do so, although I already knew, in the end, many had already made up their minds after Philipp's speech.

Philipp gave a look of disdain to his father and a final look of defiance toward me as he was immediately taken away by those charged to protect him. The thin veil of his secret supporters was fully ripped now allowing others who were so inclined, to see him truthfully.

I turned to Harry and spoke directly;

"I know that your son's words and actions have troubled you and you've got more questions than answers, but I need you to trust that Heaven is fully aware and your son is only playing a small role in what has been set into motion since the beginning of time. You, too, have a role to play and it is that conversation we need to have, now."

Without drawing any more undue attention to His Royal Highness or myself, I returned to my normal state of being, and we exited the auditorium into the late afternoon sun, entering his awaiting car before few recognized or noticed him as nothing more than a well dressed businessman. All of those departing minds of the conference were preoccupied with all they had experienced and each were more interested in rushing home to learn about the Center's grand openings in their neighborhoods and across the world.

Sitting across from the King in his luxury sedan, I looked into his eyes and saw the boy that he too used to be, the misfit of the royal family who was belligerent about living his own life. Much of that old spirit, he secretly felt he had passed along to his son and now that regret was abundantly clear in his demeanor. My next words to him would be most important in giving him a clear conscience as we moved forward to fulfill what Heaven was asking of him.

"The man that you just witnessed at that podium and backstage is no longer your son. Your continued interaction with him would not have accomplished your desired goal of getting him to return home with you, or to come to his senses.

I didn't bring you here to rescue your son.., but to sacrifice him."

My words immediately took hold of King Harry's heart as he fully grasped what I was saying.

"Sacrifice him??!! Surely you don't mean for me to kill my own son??"

"Yes, ...*we do.*"

...a Gathering of Souls

The day after Prince Philipp's call to service for everyman to play his part by pledging his mind toward the collective destruction of the threats in the sky, there was an outpouring of support globally that no one could have anticipated or predicted. What sounded like a half-baked plan to most of the learned men on the panel that day, turned into a ground swell of such unparallel support that Prince Philipp positioned himself firmly and completely as *Savior of the World* and *Time Magazine* had given him the cover to prove it.

Once those first converts entered *The Center,* they found it to be a little more intrusive than anticipated but in the midst of that much peer pressure, no one complained when they were told that needed to consent to a quick physical to ensure their mental, emotional and physical capacities, in order to receive the total support promised.

It was also explained to them that because of the unbelievable about of paperwork this global workforce would create, that a new system of accounting had to be instituted. Everything would be done from this day forward, *electronically.* With a simple *implant* that would be administered during their physicals, everyone would have a unique identification specifically coded to their DNA and with this connection, the work of connecting their minds would not only be achieved, but payments for their efforts would also be able to reach them, immediately, anywhere in the world, without the need of bank or postal service. This was met with a rousing cheer of enthusiasm in every country, and no one was the wiser that they, like Judas when he traded my brother's loyalty for 30 pieces of silver, were selling their allegiance for convenience of financial gain. Many weeks would pass before those in the religious communities realized they were witnessing the final 'sign' and that these times were indeed *the last days* and they were playing out prophetically.

All too late, they opened their bibles to Revelations 19:20 to discover that unwittingly many in their congregations had become part of the very system that would ensure their certain destruction and damnation.

19: And the beast was seized, and with him the false prophet who performed the signs in his presence, by which he deceived those who had received the mark of the beast and those who worshiped his image; these two were thrown alive into the lake of fire which burns with brimstone.

Yes, much too late for some.., *but not for all.*

~:~

EdenDust watched with particular interest the events unfold on the passing earth. He was certainly prepared to receive those souls that I gathered but intuitively felt that even this remnant of Adam would never be fully GOD's even in the new earth being presented to them. This wasn't doubt as much as it was his desire to see GOD fully worshiped in Truth. Still, he continued in his diligent obedience to make ready their new home, his beloved EDEN.

The presence of the hovering Angels beyond EDEN reminded him daily that the time was drawing near for the call to totally destroy earth. As I gathered and prepared those final souls I knew that time was quickly approaching. Soon, Jesus would make his return to earth, two millenniums later, to complete that which had begun at the beginning of time..,
to make all ONE again with our Father.

If only more truly believed that My Father's plan all alone was to give them EDEN, the ultimate place of innocence and peace. How many generations had been sacrificed trying to take possession of that which was already given to them?

Jesus gave them so much information on His first visit and even that wasn't enough to convince them to relinquish the control they cherished so deeply. I pray will succeed where He failed for I truly don't desire that any perish. I believe that more are just misguided than evil. If only they believed that they were being constantly watched over.

If only.

~:~

It took more than a little convincing of King Harry that his role in the future events was indeed God's will. I could understand the reluctance of a father to participate in the destruction of his only son, especially one that he still felt could be saved. Ultimately, I wasn't the one to convince him but Philipp himself.

In the beginning everything that Philipp said and promised was done according to his speech. For a moment, everything did seem better and every country announced an overall improvement in the good will and health of its peoples. Wars had ceased, there was no more struggle, so crimes had declined now to the point that there was no need for the justice or penal systems. The world seemed as close to a utopian society as one could have ever imagined or hoped for. But just beneath the surface, King Harry sensed that this was all too easy and under the pretense of finally becoming one of his son's advocates, he arranged a secret meeting with Philipp to truly discover that which only a father would be able to ascertain.

It was the first time Philipp had been at the Royal Palace since the eve of his Washington DC appearance. It would also be the first time he would see his father, again, after their last visit back stage. He never felt welcomed and secretly feared that if his father ever revealed his role in the murder of his uncle, all that he was building would be jeopardized. So he knew that the only way to assure his ultimate success would be to finish what he had started and take possession of the throne. Only then would he have complete power and the official title to go along with it. That evening, as Philipp entered his father's private study, he felt that he had been given the perfect opportunity to carry out his plans, as the only security was just beyond the outer offices, since the inner sanctum was considered the most protected in the palace.

While King Harry was preparing for his son's visit, he replayed our conversations about what signs to look for that would tell him that Prince Philipp was no longer to be trusted and that he had indeed become the dutiful servant of another and not the Throne of England.

I was watching all of this unfold unbeknownst to either of them from a vantage point beyond the observance of the security that was in place to avoid such electronic eavesdropping. That system only worked if electronics were being employed to invade the private quarters, but they were useless against *Spirit*. Just like my brother Jesus kept constant vigil on all of Heaven and earth, I was equally able to view all created matter in much the same way, now, for intervention as He was equipped to do, especially in those rare moments that in doing so would restore the balance. Knowing the intentions of both the hearts of King Harry and Prince Philipp had all of Heaven's attention and both of us were paying particular attention to this interaction.

Philipp entered his father's chambers and greeted him, coldly.

"I'm here, like the ever dutiful son. What was so important that I had to arrive under the dark of night?"

King Harry studied his son's countenance and truly saw nothing but a dark veil over his son's whole being. *Could it really be true, that Philipp now represented something ancient and evil?*, he thought to himself as he moved slowly toward his son to bridge the gap between them, physically and emotionally.

"First, I owe you an apology, son, I should have sought more understanding from you, than an immediate rush to judgment and my own inappropriate display of anger in that last meeting. I have watched your work.., your tireless work, from afar and have seen you do exactly what you promised that day in your speech. It would appear that none of us had the vision that only you possessed to save our world and for that I wanted to say that I am grateful for your willingness to give such a generous gift to the entire world."

Not expecting this conversation of all the ones he had planned to have with his father, for a moment, Philipp wanted to rush into his father's arms for what he expected was an appropriate embrace, but as soon as he felt that little compassion, he remembered that he hadn't been forgiven for his most heinous crime.., the death of his uncle, his father's brother. So, he just stood there, speechless. But his father had more to say and continued.

"Philipp, I think you were too young to know that although I respected my brother, William, I was always in his shadow and not just the one caused by his succession to the Throne. What you may not be fully aware of is that at one time, I was his mortal enemy and hated him as much as I think you might hate me, now."

Philipp had read all the old news accounts of the antics of his father as a young man, so this wasn't news to him, but the confession of it all was truly beyond anything he ever expected his father to so effortlessly admit. He was cautious, but spoke up.

"Father, none of this is news to me and 'tho you might not believe it, especially considering what I've done, I knew that you might not ever become King, without my intervention. So, I won't and can't apologize for accelerating that process."

"No Philipp, I don't suspect you would. And, I don't need you to. What I wanted to say to you, today, is THANK YOU for having the courage to do something I had secretly wished to do, but never had the will to carry out. If anything, I feel responsible for you ever being placed in that position to carry out what was always secretly in my heart."

So this was the moment that Heaven feared most. Not that the father would kill his son, preempting the need to fully destroy the earth, but that the son and father would join forces. My brother had advised me to never be surprised by the darkness that truly resided in the heart of man but here it was again. But, just as I thought I knew the outcome of this touching family moment.., it changed, almost instantly.

When Philipp heard that his father felt much the same, and closed the gap to seemingly embrace his father after all these years, in that moment King Harry looked into his son's eyes for a glimmer of the hope that he had championed to me that he believed was there. What he saw in Philipp's eyes, all too late, was nothing but pure contempt. His confession hadn't convinced Philipp to trust him more and return to him like the prodigal son, but in fact it caused Philipp to see him as worthless, maybe even a coward.

In that moment of coldness he felt in his son's gaze he knew that he had made a critical and tactical error in his judgment. In that moment, he asked forgiveness of me for his belligerent disbelief and told me in his spirit to do what he knew I must to not allow his son to become the murderer of any others. I in turn spoke quickly thru the Spirit to him and gave him peace in his final moments.

Philipp moved in close to his father, embracing him in one final deathly display of quiet hatred as the concealed syringe pierced the exposed vein of his father's neck. I watched my brother gather Harry's soul and embrace him into his heavenly family before passing him along to EdenDust.

King Harry's inability to sacrifice his son had now led to his own death. Ever prepared to seize a moment, Prince Philipp played the role of broken prodigal for the entire world as he recounted the call to come see his father in his inner chamber, only to arrive there, too late for their last chance at reconciliation. He read through tears, his father's *suicide* confession of killing his brother, William, for the throne and in horror and shock the world mourned for the troubled royals and freely embraced newly crowned, King Philipp, all the more.

In one fortuitous moment, he had erased his sins publicly and had accomplished the very thing that gave Heaven its final signal that the world was ready to be destroyed and that it was indeed time to gather those final souls, worth gathering.

King Philipp, *the anti-Christ*, could only be destroyed now, by the *King of Kings*.

...a Gathering of Angels

EDEN is ready.

I feel the anticipation of it all similar to those moments when I know I'm about to walk with GOD. This is an experience that I've never had, so the unknown element is imagining what the new inhabitants will think of this place, their new home..., my home. Will they have any memory of what they've left behind, or will GOD allow them a fresh beginning? I know the Holy Scriptures that others have been allowed to read speak of being reunited with loved ones, but I don't see how that can be. Even if they were here, there's nothing recognizable that would tell anyone just who another soul was on earth. The essence that creates the man is all that's here and since no one has ever seen the other's essence, I'm here to tell you it's unlike any experience they've ever had.

To be here, in the presence of GOD, is to be complete, without a shadow of doubt or an errant thought, and a freedom none of them have ever known. Just that part of it will be so overwhelmingly satisfying, I don't believe they'll ever wish for anything more. But then again, the same could have said about Adam, and look at what happened to him. But then again, that was because sin was still present the world outside the gates and this time, that won't be an issue. This time, there won't be an opportunity for that kind of intrusion. No, both Lucifer and his antichrist are going to be cast into the lake of fire.

Seemingly, right on cue, as I had that final impression, I heard Gabriel's instrument pierce the calm of Heaven. At the same time, I looked to the earth and I saw all of mankind, in every country and time zone, look to the Heavens in search of that sound.

As if rehearsed for months, the angels all focused their attention to the Throne of GOD and in particular to *Jesus*, as he arose and began to descend from the Throne.

Michael, the second most powerful angel in Heaven appeared in the distance on what could only be described in earthly terms as a powerful white horse, but in truth, it's a creature that only exists in Heaven and it's 1000 times more powerful than your stealth bombers and swifter than the speed of thought.

As Jesus descended Heaven, he appeared to those on earth as if He were standing on Mount Zion, just beyond the Mount of Olives in Jerusalem. From any direction in the world, this image of Christ on the Mount Zion and the preceding trumpet blast meant that the prophecy of scripture was truly and finally being fulfilled.

At the moment of His appearing, all over the world the oceans disappeared and if one looked out, it appeared as if the earth was devoid of water and in the place of where there had been oceans, the most *terrible beasts* that one could possibly imagine appeared on the horizons all led by the one called the *Dragon* that we knew as Lucifer before he was cast down to earth. Their images were so terrifying that many dropped dead where they stood while others, for fear of being killed and eaten alive, fell down to worship the Dragon who seemed to command the beasts that rose from the depth of the seas.

Christ stood on that mount for a season while the whole world went mad. All that time they had spent, putting their collective minds to work, ended up being as useless as Damon had predicted. Even though King Philipp had been led to believe his own lies, he now found himself playing second fiddle to the Dragon that had obviously proven in these final days to be as deceitful as he had always been to those that learned all too late that the only agenda he was interested in *was his own.*

The streets ran freely with the blood of those that had received the mark that foolishly they thought was for their good and necessary for their financial futures. Few knew that it made them an easily assessable target and unfit for salvation at the time they needed it most. A *lucky* few ended their own lives, realizing all too late that everything that they had thought was 'make believe' when they scoffed at the tele-evangelists, was indeed true. While those that turned their backs on King Philipp's plan made their way to the foot of Mount Zion, that chosen 144,000, many millions more were lost to eternal damnation for their shortsightedness and vanity. And, while others were being sealed and were safely in the presence of EdenDust, being prepared for the new earth, so many more would be lost, forever.

Finally, with just a glance, Michael appeared before the throne and Jesus took his rightful place on his chariot and led the charge from Heaven with the Legions of Angels in tow.

I wish I could adequately describe what total destruction looks like, but Angels unleashed to do that which only they can ever fully do is beyond descriptive words. The screams of the tormented lasted for a full month, night and day. Every living soul, including four legged beasts and foul of the air, were utterly destroyed. At the end of this complete decimation, only the Dragon, Lucifer and his antichrist, King Philipp, were left standing, each being spared for the only One that truly possessed the power to destroy them. In one cumulative motion, Jesus grabbed them both and cast them down into the bowels of the earth, their eternal resting place, to be tormented for eternity.

Almost immediately, there was silence on the face of the whole earth and those very Angels that had just fulfilled their destructive roles with such authority, lifted their voices and begin to sing in the most beautiful tones ever, heralding the coming of GOD and the new earth, for the old one had truly passed away.

...a New Earth

1. **Then I saw a new heaven and a new earth; for the first heaven and the first earth passed away, and there is no longer any sea. 2. And I saw the holy city, New Jerusalem, coming down out of Heaven from GOD, made ready as a bride adorned for her husband. 3. And I heard a loud voice from the Throne, saying, "Behold, the tabernacle of GOD is among men, and He will dwell among them. 4. And He shall wipe away every tear from their eyes; and there will no longer be any death; there will no longer be any mourning, or crying, or pain; the first things have passed away."**

This scene, so aptly described by John in Revelation 21 is the only mention of *me* in the whole bible.., and though I'm not called by name, this was the honor My Father bestowed upon me, *the pronouncement of the new earth*. The voice that John heard decreeing all that would be and the passage of all that was, was my own, ***EdenDust.***

As caretaker of EDEN, *the new earth*, the honor was bestowed upon me to present this new Jerusalem, this new home that translates to mean Wholeness and Peace, to those that GOD has saved from utter destruction.

After my sacred prelude, John was allowed to see the rest of the vision that is *now* actually taking place.

5. He was seated on the Throne said "I am making everything new!" Then He said, "Write this down, for these words are trustworthy and true." 6. He said to me; "I AM the Alpha and the Omega, the Beginning and the End. To him who is thirsty I will give drink without cost from the Spring of the Water of Life. 7. He who overcomes will inherit all this, and I will be his GOD and he will be my Son.

What a glorious day this is!!

My Father is now fully present in EDEN and He's permanently bridged the chasm between Heaven and the New Earth.

Everything beyond this moment is new.
It has never been seen, there is nothing recorded, as it is all happening NOW, for the first time.

Oh what JOY floods my Soul !!!

BOOK FOUR
Prologue:

To give you a full accounting of the time since the end of the old world and the beginning of the New Earth, it would take a new vocabulary, one that I certainly possess, since I've been in charge of creating it, but not one that I'm permitted to fully reveal, at this time. Just know for the record, that this isn't a secret place nor a place of pure fantasy, but one that is certainly going to happen, *in your lifetime*.

Remember, I know things. I've seen your future and this little story is nothing more than a foreshadowing of things to come. Now that you're aware, it's your responsibility to consider your present role in the unfolding of this reality. And, when you're ready to be fully awakened, just come back to this author for I know he's dying to reveal all the rest that I've shown him, alone, if there's enough interest in knowing GOD's will for each of you that's taken the time to read this first offering.

The heavenly hosts are singing hosannas *now* and that can only mean **GOD** is on the throne and my time with you must come to an end. I pray we will gather again, together like this, soon ...but that isn't fully up to me, is it?

I pray you *Shalom..*, nothing missing and nothing broken.., and that you'll allow your soul to be kept in Perfect Peace until we get to meet for the first time.

Thank you for reading my words.

Made in the USA
Charleston, SC
25 June 2013